# Murder in Palo Alto

The condo developer wasn't known for her community spirit, but that was no reason to push her out of a third-story window, or to dispose of her in a dumpster. Housewife/writer Bridget Montrose, who discovers the body, reluctantly pursues clues through Palo Alto from behind a stroller. She uncovers suburban goings-on that really belong in the dumpster, as the mystery spreads to involve friends, neighbors, and some surprisingly simpatico cops. By the time she finally tracks down the truth, the murderer's right behind her . . .

in a real Revolting Development

Lora R. Smith

# Revolting Development

A *mystery* from **Perseverance Press**
*Menlo Park, California*

Art direction by Gary Page/Merit Media.
Photography by Rob Egashira/Fabrizio Camera Graphics.
Shoes courtesy of Rapp's, Palo Alto.
Typography by Jim Cook/Book Design & Typography.

Published by
Perseverance Press
P.O. Box 384
Menlo Park, California 94026

Manufactured in the United States of America.

This book is printed on acid-free paper.

2  3  —  90  89

Library of Congress Catalog Card Number 87-72895

ISBN: 0-9602676-6-2

*To all of you out there—*
*you know who you are.*

AUTHOR'S NOTE

*There is, of course, a real Palo Alto, with real people living in it. But the Palo Alto and its inhabitants who appear in this book are from an alternative universe, where much is similar but nothing is the same. None of the people in this book exist in real life, and even the institutions, such as the police department, are the author's imaginary vision of what might possibly be happening in that alternative universe. The author would be happy to think her characters have enough vitality to be considered real, but they do not, in actual fact, bear any resemblance to anyone—living, dead, or otherwise.*

Revolting
Development

# Prologue

MARGERY LOMAX DROPPED her spoon into her soup plate. A small fleck of gold chipped off the rim, and she stared at it for a moment before fixing her gaze on her husband, separated from her by eight feet of shining mahogany. The chipped plate was just one more thing to be laid at his door.

Fred pretended to ignore her displeasure, but she knew he knew. When his Adam's apple bobbed like that he was nervous. And with good cause.

"I simply do not understand it," Margery said, tapping well-polished talons on the table. Usually the sight of her hands brought a glow of good humor. She considered them quite elegant and young-looking, for a woman of her years. Not that she was growing old—no, she was timeless. Everyone agreed. She wished she could say the same of Fred. He was looking all of his fifty-eight years lately. It was no wonder.

"You have acted very foolishly, Fred," she told him. "Gambling is not your forte—you must have recognized that by now. How did you think you were going to pay these debts?"

Fred looked down at the dregs of his tomato soup. "I hoped—I didn't like to ask you," he mumbled.

"Well, you should have. Now it will cost me three times as much to get you out of it as it would have if you'd come to me in the first place." She reached for her water glass and noticed that her hand was trembling. It was bad for her to

1

get so angry. The doctor had said she must learn to remain calm. "But what provocation," she thought, taking a ladylike sip of water and striving to regain control.

"Margy—" Fred's Adam's apple was really hopping, she noticed. "I'm cured of gambling. I'll never gamble again."

"You may be sure of that," Mrs. Lomax said, staring down the table at him. Really, he positively repelled her, with his watery eyes and thinning hair. Why had she ever married a man so weak? "If I decide to bail you out of this mess, and I do mean if, I shall arrange to have the casinos closed to you in the future." She pushed the soup plate away. "There won't be any difficulty about that, I imagine, when I let it be known that I won't be responsible for your debts."

"You—you must pay it for me." Fred's eyes bulged with alarm. "They—they threatened—"

Mrs. Lomax got up and went to the sideboard, where the housekeeper had left the casserole in a chafing dish. "Be a man, Fred," she said impatiently over her shoulder. "They can't do more than break your arms and legs, and you certainly deserve it for such stupid, sneaky behavior." She scooped up a spoonful of the casserole and added plenty of broccoli. Broccoli was supposed to be good for you. "Be sure you take some broccoli, Fred. And stop sniveling. I suppose I'll pay your debt—this time."

They finished their meal in silence. Mrs. Lomax didn't like to feel that there was a quality of resentment in her husband's behavior. After all, she was rescuing him from unpleasantness at the hands of the casino enforcers. The magnitude of his deception rather astonished her. Daring to gamble at Lake Tahoe, when she'd sent him to check on the possibility of building some condominiums at Fallen Leaf Lake! It wasn't like Fred to be so independent.

A thought occured to her over the gelatin parfait. "And how did your secretary enjoy the lake? Miss—Miss Arrow, is it?"

"Miss Dart," Fred said sullenly, his eyes shifting away from hers. "She—she was working on the contracts."

"Of course she was," Mrs. Lomax cooed. "It probably took all her time. Poor thing, she's not too efficient, besides being so odd-looking. I think I will find you someone else, Freddy."

"Allison—Miss Dart is a fine legal secretary." Fred clenched his fists. Mrs. Lomax watched him narrowly. "You must allow me to hire my own office help, Margy."

"Must I?" She laughed. "Come, Freddy. Don't look so glum. If I'm going to buy you out of your little fix, the least you can do is hire a new secretary to please me. Someone mature," she added, clasping her hands girlishly. "And very competent. I'll see to it for you, shall I?"

Fred's shoulders slumped. "Certainly," he said, his voice hollow.

"Then that's settled. Now I've got a planning commission meeting to attend, and afterward I want to go around and check those units on Wadsworth. Mr. Neary is not making the kind of progress I expect on my construction sites."

Fred stood up when she did, abandoning the rest of his dinner. "You're a little old to go climbing around a half-finished building in the middle of the night, Margy. Leave it till tomorrow."

She stiffened at his mention of age and led the way out of the dining room. "I won't go alone, Freddy, since you're so concerned. I plan to have some company." Her lips tightened. Fred wasn't the only recalcitrant person she had to deal with tonight. But she was confident that all these annoying people could be brought under control. All it took was the right bit of knowledge . . . "That Kaplan woman," she muttered to herself.

"What? Claudia Kaplan? You're taking her on a tour of your condos?"

"Don't be more of a moron than you can help, Fred." She got her coat out of the closet under the stairs, stroking the soft mink with affection. It was cold in Palo Alto at this time of year. Briefly she toyed with the idea of Palm Springs. But the development restrictions were even tighter there. "Mrs.

Kaplan will no doubt show up at the meeting. I'm afraid her
so-called literary reputation gives her weight with the planning commission. I need a good handle against her, and so
far I haven't found one."

Fred was unable to conceal a faint smile of satisfaction.
"So you can't make her dance to your tune. Or that other
fellow—what's his name? Hippie type."

"You mean Martin Hertschorn, I suppose." Mrs. Lomax
felt a scowl forming and forced her facial muscles into
slackness. No reason to court wrinkles, after all. "He has no
real influence, but these gadflies can be very annoying.
However, I shall prevail."

"Of course." Fred looked apprehensive. "You won't—say
anything that would leave you open to an action for slander,
will you? I barely got the last one bought off."

For a moment she let her anger with Fred relax into
approval. After all, he had his uses. It seemed unfair that it
should be slanderous simply to point out venal flaws in
others. And it was true that something occasionally came
over her, and she would find herself saying things, hurling
words that normally weren't part of her vocabulary. The last
time she'd aired a difference of opinion with Mrs. Kaplan,
she'd had a hard time stopping herself from abandoning
decorum and shrieking "dyke-lover, dyke-lover." The
memory of that hot engulfing darkness made her reach for a
package of tissues.

"Maybe I should come with you," Fred offered. There
was reluctance in the words. He had one eye on his watch,
she noticed. Some television program he wanted to watch.

"Unnecessary, Fred," Mrs. Lomax said briskly. "If anyone
commits slander tonight, it'll be Claudia Kaplan. She was
very threatening after the last meeting, but not in front of
witnesses, unfortunately." Mrs. Lomax sniffed. "I, of course,
will maintain complete control." She pressed down those
unquiet memories and shot Fred a withering glance to show
that her anger was not forgotten. "Over my family, it seems

I have no control. You are a disappointment to me, Fred, a bitter disappointment. And my nephew is not much better."

Fred brightened. "Young MacIntyre got himself into trouble?"

"It seems I am only useful to both of you as a walking pocket book. It must come to an end." Mrs. Lomax picked up her briefcase and headed for the door. "If Benji thinks I will subsidize his foolish passion for bicycle racing, he has a surprise coming." She turned for a last glare at Fred. "And that's not all I refuse to subsidize. Good night, my dear. I shall be late. Don't wait up."

# 1

"NOW, EXACTLY WHERE were you when you saw the feet?" Bridget Montrose shivered and wrapped herself in her sweatshirted arms. The early morning air was as cold and damp as a child's unwrung washcloth. "Please, Sig. I'd rather not have to go through it all again."

Since Signe Harrison was her dearest friend, Bridget knew she wouldn't take no for an answer. Squinting against the weak morning light, Signe was tall, pale of face with pale brown hair, thin, her expression eager and quivering, cultivated for its pathos. Using it, she never failed to get at least one more nugget of information out of her victim.

Most of the time Bridget found this amusing. But this morning she was the victim. Sig's recent ambition was to jump from the local weekly paper to one of the bigger peninsula dailies. Consequently her nose for news had grown, Pinocchio-like, to immense proportions.

"Listen, this is a big break for me." Sig turned the pathos way up. "Why else do you think I barreled right over here when I heard your name on the police band?"

"Everyone else in Palo Alto listens to *Morning Edition* while they eat their granola." Bridget made an effort to sound normal, though she felt as if she would never stop shivering. The wet February wind pierced right through her sweaty clothes. She was dressed to move, not to stand around trying to avoid watching a corpse get loaded into an ambulance. "The Lois Lane of our time," she said, turning

6

her back on the ambulance and clenching her teeth so they wouldn't chatter. "This is not going to look good on the Community Activities page."

"What Community Activities? This could be my ticket out of the *Crier*." Sig pointed her razor-point pen right at Bridget's heart. "My best friend finds a body in a dumpster! You have to tell me about it, Biddy." She played her trump card. "After all, you told that wimp from the *Peninsula Times*. I saw you talking to him earlier."

Bridget capitulated, as she had known she would. They were standing in front of the Dark Tower, her private name for the condominiums-to-be that had replaced her favorite Victorian mansion near downtown Palo Alto. The usual muddy desolation of a construction site that she jogged past every day was overrun on this morning with police cars and people both official and unofficial, slogging through the mud, peering at everything. Occasionally Bridget caught furtive glances and mutterings in her direction. She felt branded by lurid speculation.

"I was running along the sidewalk," she began mournfully, reciting it all for the umpteenth time. "Coming from my house. It was early, still pretty dark out, but the streetlight happened to reflect off the soles of the shoes just right."

The words caught in her throat and she knew she would never be able to forget the whole bizarre scene. "They were sticking straight up out of the dumpster—really nice Italian shoes, you know the kind, impossibly high heels with light-colored waxed leather soles. Must have been pretty new because they were still shiny. I don't run that fast, you know—" she glared at Sig's unrepressed snort of laughter "—so while I was going past I had time to realize that they actually were shoes and not just weird shadows or something."

She took a deep breath and so did Sig. "Not too clear," Sig said, writing furiously in a small notebook, "but I get your drift."

"Well, I started to go on, figuring it was just a joke, or

some street art or something." Bridget fingered the zipper
tab on her sweatshirt. "I really don't know what made me go
through all that mud to check it out."

The mud had been unpleasantly clingy after a couple of
wet days, and her thoughts had been diverted from the
strange appearance of the dumpster to the fear that the mud
would ruin her expensive new running shoes. She almost
turned back at that point, but another glance at the dumpster
that stood in the shadow of the new building changed her
mind.

She had stopped short, nearly sinking to her hocks in the
mud. From her closer vantage, it was clear that the shoes
were being worn. Thin stocking-clad legs were visible up to
mid-calf level, apparently being disgorged by the dumpster.
Presumably the legs themselves were attached to knees, and
so on. The refrain of an old song had begun running through
her shocked mind, and she could still feel it at the edge of her
consciousness, ready to come spilling out if she didn't
exercise enough control. "Knee bone connected to the—
thigh bone, thigh bone connected to the—hip bone . . ." Had
she said it out loud? She looked anxiously at Sig, and decided
she had not, so far.

"Anyway, that's it. I banged on the door of the next house
and called nine one one and the next thing I knew—" she
gestured around at the crowd of police, ambulance workers,
and unnamed extras.

"She was dead when they pulled her out?" Sig nodded,
answering her own question, and scribbled some more.
"Margery Lomax," she muttered. "Hoist in her own
development."

Both of them looked up at the Dark Tower, where a sign
in one staring, glassless window proclaimed: EIGHT LUXURY
CONDOMINIUM UNITS AVAILABLE SOON. MARGERY
LOMAX, DEVELOPER.

Bridget shivered again. "Every morning when I run past
this monstrosity I have bad thoughts about her. Now she's
dead."

At least Sig didn't write that down. She put her notebook away and threw a long, comforting arm around Bridget's quivering shoulders. "Why are you hanging around here? Emery must be frantic."

"I called him," Bridget mumbled. "The police said I should stick around for a while."

"Well, they can find you again if they want you. You need something warm to drink. Bet you're still in shock."

Bridget let Sig lead her away. The heavy grey sky lightened fractionally, signaling that the sun was on the job somewhere up there. Despite the cold, gloomy wetness of the atmosphere, buds on the Japanese plum trees lining the street were beginning to swell. A breeze off the Bay carried the faint, pleasant tang of salt water. It would be spring again soon, with the breathtaking suddenness that vindicated the nasty chill of the winter rains. But Margery Lomax would see no more springs.

They had nearly reached Sig's car when a voice hailed them. "Ladies!" Bridget turned to see a man coming toward them from the Dark Tower, picking a way with surprising swiftness through the clingy mud. As he came closer she noted that he was medium height, a few inches taller than she was, stocky but compact, with fair, wildly curling hair receding from a broad forehead. He wore the kind of wire-rims that had been popular in the Sixties, and a rumpled sportcoat above faded Levis.

His eyes moved back and forth between Bridget and Sig, stopping at Bridget's face. "So you're the one who got us all out of bed early this morning. Mrs. Montrose?"

Bridget nodded.

"I'm Detective Drake of the Palo Alto police department." He glanced down at a sheaf of papers that spilled untidily from his hands. "I probably have your statement here somewhere, but I'd like to talk to you if you don't mind."

Bridget's legs started trembling, as if she'd run twice as far as usual instead of half as far. "Can it wait? My family—"

"In an investigation of this kind we like to get moving as fast as we can."

"Which kind is it?" Sig's voice was eager. "Is it—murder?"

"Don't be silly, Sig." Bridget leaned against the car. "She probably had a heart attack . . ." That was stupid. Heart attack victims rarely tidied themselves away. "Why was she in the dumpster?"

Drake watched her, the lenses of his wire-rims catching the weak light and flinging it back. "That's what we need to find out, Mrs. Montrose. Do you have a few minutes?"

Bridget's teeth chattered like castanets. "Are you saying she *was* murdered?" Speaking the word brought an atavistic fear boiling to the surface of her mind. She barely felt Sig give her a comforting hug. "There's a murderer running around here." She turned to Sig. "I want to go home now. Emery—the children—I want to go home."

"Now, now, Mrs. Montrose." Lt. Drake flicked his eyes over her, and she imagined him calculating how long it would be before she collapsed. "I wouldn't worry, ma'am. With your cooperation, we'll have this all cleaned up in no time."

Bridget decided it was all a dream, one of those particularly vivid dreams where you noticed things like the heavy clang of ambulance doors shutting, and the color of the sky, as grey as tapioca cooked in an aluminum pot. The sky began to waver. Sig's indignant voice came from far away.

"She's going to faint! Why don't you let her go home and pull herself together? It isn't every day a person finds a body, you know."

Bridget took three deep breaths. "I'm not going to faint," she said. Her voice came out squeaky. She realized her eyes were closed, and opened them. Detective Drake was watching her. She didn't like the intensity in his gaze. He turned his attention to the papers he held, shuffling through them and pulling one out.

"I've got your address here," he said, waving the scrap and cramming it into his pocket. "My partner or I will stop by later today." He nodded to Sig and loped back toward the Dark Tower.

Sig looked after him, speculative. "Abrupt sort of guy. Wonder if he's married."

Bridget began to laugh and then, uncontrollably, to cry. "I want to go home," she managed to gasp. "Please, Sig—"

"Of course, honey." Sig bustled her into the car, but her eyes returned to the distant figure of Lt. Drake. "Good looking guy, anyway. Maybe I should interview him for the paper."

# 2

DETECTIVE PAUL DRAKE plodded back through the mud to the dumpster, cramming papers into his pockets as he went. The ambulance pulled away, its wheels splattering a gout of mud that eliminated the last clean spot on his ancient Converse high-tops.

Bruno Morales, his partner, looked up from a study of the ground near the dumpster when Paul stopped beside him. "Why couldn't this have waited until after the rainy season?" Bruno's face was creased with distress around his anxious brown eyes. He was a couple of years younger than Paul's thirty-eight, still taking the weight of the world on his shoulders. "Why do people have to get bumped off in the worst possible places?"

"At least the killer was neat," Paul pointed out, squinting in turn at the churned-up ground around the dumpster. All the investigators kept scrupulously to the far side of the area cordoned off by the uniformed officers who had responded to the first call. "Disposed of the body properly, you might say."

Bruno looked reproachful. "You got no respect, Paolo. You shouldn't be flippant about death."

Paul let that pass. "So what do you make of it?" He noticed a couple of tracks at one side of the dumpster. Rainwater had collected in the deepest part of them.

"For starters, we got size twelve, thirteen hiking boots—there's the trace of a lug sole. From the depth of the water in

them, those prints were made around three a.m. But here's
the funny thing." Bruno tugged on his arm and led him
around the side of the looming building. "More prints of
hiking boots—clearer this time. And they were made days—
maybe weeks ago."

Paul stared down at the prints. This side of the building
was invisible from the street. An ancient live oak defied the
construction site, drooping its branches to within feet of the
ground. The prints, sheltered by the oak, were smudged but
still discernable.

"Why do you think they're old? They might have been
made last night too."

Bruno's voice was patient. "Use your eyes, Paolo. It was
done long enough ago that a cat has walked across the prints
and the sun has dried them. We've had no sun for five days
now, so I'm guessing these prints were made during that last
spell of good weather we had."

Paul scratched his head. His partner's Sherlockian expertise was something of a legend in the department. But he still
wasn't convinced about the footprints.

"There's lots of hiking boots around. These were probably
made by someone else—one of the construction crew," he
suggested.

"Maybe. But I got a feeling." Bruno thumped his chest,
and Paul sighed. He believed in Bruno's feelings, which were
correct more often than not, but found them hard to justify
in the investigative reports.

Bruno led the way back to the front of the building. A
crowd of bathrobed neighbors hovered at the sidewalk,
behind the chain link fence that enclosed the front of the site.
Construction workers had begun to show up, and were
being interviewed by a uniformed patrolwoman.

"Here's something else we found." Bruno stopped at
another cordoned-off area that encompassed a few feet of
the terrazzo pavement surrounding the building. He lifted a
plastic tarp and pointed to an almost indiscernable dark
splotch on the edge of the pavement. The mud beneath the

tarp held an indentation, just about large enough to cradle a slight woman's body.

Paul whistled softly and looked up at the gaping window holes, at the roof edge three stories above them. Bruno followed his gaze. "That's what we figure," he said, managing to include the other personnel in his royal we. "Came off the upper story, landed right here, cracked her skull on the edge of the pavement. There was a wound on the back of her head that would fit that scenario. She might not have died if she'd fallen farther into the mud."

"Fell—or was pushed?"

"That's the question, isn't it?"

Paul pushed his glasses higher on his nose and stared at the depression in the muddy earth, and then at the dumpster, a matter of 50 feet away. "So having fallen or been pushed, how did Mrs. Lomax get into the dumpster?"

"That's the other question."

Rhea Horton, the policewoman, came up to them, accompanied by a middle-aged man dressed in work clothes and lace-up boots. His shirt buttons strained over a truly majestic beer belly. "This is Mr. Neary," she said. Paul pulled his fascinated gaze away from the belly. "He's the construction crew foreman. He says Mrs. Lomax did have a habit of visiting her developments at all hours."

"That's right," Mr. Neary confirmed. "I told her a thousand times she was asking for trouble. Tell you the truth, I didn't like it at all. She'd come out at midnight, poke around—next day there'd be a big list tacked up to the door frame—why wasn't I doing this? Why did I do that?" He shrugged and inserted a hairy finger between the gaping buttons of his shirt, scratching luxuriously. "Why did she stick her nose in so much, that's what I wanted to know. Always tryin' to teach me my business." He paused and took off his bright yellow hard hat, holding it over his heart as if ready to say the pledge of allegiance. "Rest in peace, of course," he added.

Paul and Bruno exchanged glances. "Was there a note this morning?"

Bruno shook his head.

"Interrupted by death," Mr. Neary said with relish. "And speaking of interruptions, when can we get back in here?"

Paul shrugged. "The police investigation will take a few more hours. If significant evidence turns up, we may ask the court to halt construction for a time. Do you happen to know who would take over her projects?"

Mr. Neary scratched his head before clapping his hard hat back on. "No idea. Are you sayin' we might as well go home?" He frowned at Paul.

"That's really up to you, Mr. Neary."

Gloomily Mr. Neary took his hard hat off again. "Guess I won't be needing this today."

Bruno spoke up suddenly. "Would she—would Mrs. Lomax have gone into the construction site without a hard hat?"

Mr. Neary looked at Bruno in amazement. "Hell, no." He made a few preliminary noises and spat. "Had her own hard hat, personalized and everything. Liked to get her picture taken wearing it. Never went into the site without it."

Bruno shook his head, answering Paul's question before he asked it. "Nobody's found any trace of such a thing so far." He loped over to consult with the men who were going through the dumpster.

"Can I go now?" Mr. Neary's voice was plaintive. Paul wrote down his phone number and waved him away. Bruno came back, with Rhea Horton.

"They're down to the little stuff in the bottom of the dumpster. No hard hat."

"Maybe she left it at home," Rhea suggested. She was young and enthusiastic, pleasant to look at—not too skinny, Paul thought. Her cheerful face was unusually vindictive. "Maybe she was tipsy after a party or something, came along to visit her baby condos, staggered up to the top floor and lost her balance." Rhea smacked a fist into her palm. "Splat!"

Paul and Bruno stared at her. "Ms. Horton," Bruno said finally.

Rhea colored. "Sorry. I didn't know Mrs. Lomax, of course. But the first apartment Jimmy and I had together was in the old house that used to be here. It was a beautiful place." She stared around at the angular planes of the condos in progress. "This is hardly an improvement."

Bruno moved forward and put a gentle arm around Rhea's shoulders. "Thanks for interviewing the neighbors for us, Ms. Horton. Could you go write it up now? And then I think we can release you. We've almost wrapped it up here."

Rhea stalked off. "I can't really blame her," Paul said. "This place gives me the heebee-jeebies. What did Mrs. Montrose call it in her statement, the Dark Tower?"

"She's the one who found the body." Bruno pulled a calculator out of his pocket and began to punch little buttons with lightning speed. "Did you go over her statement with her?"

"Not yet." Paul stared at Bruno's fingers. "Is this any time to balance your checkbook?"

"Huh?" Bruno pressed a button and a tiny card covered with figures slid out of the calculator. "I'm just figuring terminal velocity. This place is built right up to the fifty foot height limit. So depending on what they find at the autopsy, it should be possible to figure out where she fell from— second story, third story, or roof."

"Good grief." Paul ran his hands through his hair. "What next? Will we all have to bring computers to work or something? Let's go look at the roof and see if we can tell the old-fashioned way."

"Right." Bruno grinned amiably. "This terminal velocity stuff goes over big with the DA, though. Besides, it gives me an excuse to use my physics."

"Take my advice," Paul grumbled, leading the way into the building. "Physics can be dangerous. Better to leave it at home while you're working."

"You're just jealous," Bruno said complacently, "because

you don't have any physics. You should try some night-school classes, Paolo. They broaden your base of knowledge."

"Knowledge schmoledge." Paul paused at the rough stairs that circled the interior of the building. "Are we using that fancy equipment from the county—the fumer, or whatever? And if so, have they printed the railings yet?"

"I sent the guys up to the roof first," Bruno admitted. "Guess they're working their way down."

The two men climbed carefully, staying on the edges of the steps, not using the railing. "It's going to be a bitch," Paul said suddenly. "Construction crew, potential buyers, real estate agents—we won't get anything usable."

"We might." Bruno was unperturbed at the vast amount of documentation that opened before them. "We'll need physical evidence before we can nail anybody."

Paul climbed on, automatically scanning every tread before he stepped on it, and thinking about coffee—how he hadn't had any yet. If only people would confine their crimes to office hours! Then a man could be shaven, alert, with blood sugar well stoked up for the day. His stomach rumbled.

On the third floor, one of the evidence team members called them into an unfinished apartment. The floor was a series of boards laid across joists, with here and there some solid subflooring in place. Electrical wiring and plumbing pipes sprouted from the floor and walls. The evidence team was working by one of the big holes in the outer wall that would someday be windows.

"This is the place," Tim Bukowski said, straightening cheerfully and waving a small sable brush at them. "She went out of this window—stake my reputation on it."

"So much for terminal velocity," Paul muttered to Bruno. He tried not to get too close to the gaping window hole. Heights made him nervous.

"The barriers are in place at all the other windows," Tim explained, pointing to long, sawhorse-like things that had been pushed back into the room. "Here they were removed. We found some tufts of fur caught in the rough framing that match the coat she was wearing. You see any tracks, Bruno?"

Bruno was already crouched near the window, studying marks on the floor so faint that Paul had to clean his glasses before he could see them.

"Mrs. Lomax's shoes," Bruno announced after a minute. "She had small feet—size five or six. And someone else—I can't quite make it out—"

"Hiking boots?" Paul knelt beside the tracks. They looked like nothing to him. Some geometric shapes—a triangle surmounting a dot; some circles and lines. Everything was blurry and faded-looking.

"Not hiking boots." Bruno sounded puzzled. "Something else—not baseball shoes . . ."

Paul stayed low as he backed away. That gaping window spelled vertigo to him. "So she must have been on her own two feet, not carried up or anything. She moved the barrier—or someone else did—and then fell, jumped, or was pushed out the window. Any sign of her hard hat?"

Tim shook his head. "No hats of any kind. We'll get some pictures of whatever that is, if it photographs."

"Let's get going," Paul urged Bruno. "Did anyone notify next-of-kin?"

They went back down the stairs, not so carefully this time. "I sent Neal Rucker over to her house," Bruno said, scrutinizing the treads before putting his feet on them. Paul couldn't see much reason to be careful; the treads were covered in dusty, flaky, ground-in mud. "He's supposed to look around for any appointment books and diaries he can find, as well as talk to her husband. We'll have to go over there, you know."

"Let's wait until this afternoon. I want to go back to the office, touch base with Neal, and see Mrs. Montrose. Told her I would come by this morning," he added innocently. He had liked the look of Mrs. Montrose. Even shaken and pale from the trauma of her discovery, she looked cuddly. Fluffy brown hair, nice rounded body—too rounded for many men, but he had a secret preference for warm and ample women. Besides being very comfortable in bed, they usually were whizzes around the kitchen. He wasn't married any more, and couldn't afford the kind of restaurant food he liked. A woman who could cook took on added glamour.

"We'll go together, of course," Bruno said. Paul saw the smile he was imperfectly concealing. "It wouldn't be proper to let a single guy like you interview her alone."

"Look, the woman has a family around—she said so! I'm not going to seduce her, for heaven's sake. I just need to verify her statement."

"Nice big woman like that, probably has fresh-baked coffee cake every morning!" Bruno rolled his eyes in simulated ecstasy. "Probably grinds her own coffee beans for every pot! Probably has real cream in the pitcher instead of skim milk like the skinny women have—"

"Stow it, Morales." Bruno had been his partner long enough to find out his weaknesses as far as women were concerned. Paul grinned sheepishly. "What's the harm in a cup of coffee? That rotgut at the office savages my stomach lining."

Bruno looked sententious. "As my old grandmother used to say—"

"Is this your Italian grandmother again?"

"No, the one from Sonora." Bruno frowned at him. "She said, *'No se deje dar gato por liebre.'* Take it to heart, Paolo."

"Now, how am I supposed to do that?" Paul snorted. "No comprende, señor."

"Loosely translated, it means, don't get mixed up with the witnesses." Bruno shook a finger at him.

"I *know* that." Paul pushed the finger aside and squelched to his car. "Meet you at three to go see Lomax."

# 3

EMERY WAS JITTERING by the door when Bridget climbed out of Sig's car. "For God's sake, where have you been? I couldn't make head nor tail of you on the phone. Corky's late for school, I'm late for work, Sam's late for pre-school—"

Bridget smiled wanly. "Sorry, love. I told you, I found a body."

"Incredible!" Emery took her by the shoulders and shook her gently before giving her a hug. "I couldn't believe it!" He let her go so he could wave his arms around, striding into the bedroom to bring out a quilt. He tucked the quilt briskly around her, plumped her onto the couch, and scooped up Mick from the floor. "You look frozen! I can't believe this kind of thing happens! Think you're living in goddamned suburbia and the next thing you know—Hitsville!" He settled Mick into her arms. Bridget hugged the baby's warmth gratefully. "Now tell me about it! But only the G-rated parts!"

Bridget looked at Corky's open mouth, at Sam's round eyes. It wasn't safe to spell words these days, since Corky had entered first grade. Careful of the little ears, she and Sig told the story to Emery in stereo.

He heard it while getting the boys zipped into their jackets, lunch boxes at the ready. "She probably had a heart attack, just like you said," he announced at the end of it. "Margery Lomax was a Type A personality if I ever saw one.

Such a prominent woman, no wonder the police are checking into it carefully."

"I think it's fishy," Sig said ominously while Emery marshalled the children to the door. Bridget squeezed Mick and said nothing.

"Wonder if they're ready for condominiums in heaven." Emery gave Mick a loud kiss, and tossed one Bridget's way. "Got to rush. Will you be okay? Want me to cancel my afternoon meetings?"

"No, no." Bridget felt her voice lacked conviction. "I'll be perfectly fine. I doubt the police really suspect me of doing Mrs. Lomax in."

Emery laughed heartily. "If they arrest you, I'll round up all the insects you've refused to swat in the past ten years and bring them to your defense. So long, honey. I'll call you later." He shooed the older boys out the door.

"Was the body dead? Who deaded it?" They could hear Sam's high little voice before Emery got him stowed in the car. Bridget stared at Sig.

"That's the question, isn't it?"

Sig shrugged. "If it is murder, which I for one doubt, they probably know already. Either that, or they'll never find out. I don't think the police bother to detect any more. If it's not obvious right away, they just file and forget."

Bridget was shocked. "Surely not. That nice Detective Drake—"

Sig's eyes gleamed. "I'd better get back and check with him to see if it's a homicide. I'll just fix you a cup of tea—"

"Don't bother." Bridget knew she sounded pitiful. But it was pleasant to be the one bustled over for a change. She cast off the quilt and moved to the rocker that occupied a bay window near the round oak kitchen table. Mick started grizzling and she absently pulled up her sweatshirt to offer him her breast. "Detective Drake'll be coming by later, of course," she said with cunning. "You'd be sure to catch him if you just stayed here."

"There is that." Sig rinsed the teapot meticulously in

enough hot water to wash a load of diapers. She was a fanatic about tea. "I'll stay for a few minutes, anyway. Daresay you could use some company. Got any Prince of Wales?"

Bridget smiled in relief. Despite the brave front she'd put on for Emery, she didn't feel like being left alone with only a year-old baby for company. "In a can? No, I let him out." Wild giggles welled up in her throat.

"Still in shock." Sig shook her head. She picked up the tin of Twining's English Breakfast and sniffed it suspiciously. "You must have had this stuff for a thousand years."

"I've carried it with me through every previous incarnation."

"I'll get you some decent tea some time." This was a familiar threat. Sig poured boiling water into the pot, stirred three ritual times and wrapped the teapot in a towel. "And a tea cosy. I saw some cute ones at the London House."

"Just get me a cup of tea before I die and I'll be content." Mick disconnected with a loud pop and plucked demandingly at her sweatshirt. Sighing, Bridget switched him to the other side.

"I thought you were weaning him."

"I am." The doorbell sounded with an asthmatic wheeze, saving her from further argument. "Get the door, will you?"

It wasn't Detective Drake after all. It was Melanie Dixon, whose daughter attended Sam's pre-school. She said hello to Sig and joined them at the kitchen table, her slightly protrudent blue eyes bulging with excitement. "I talked to Emery when he dropped off Sam. He said you found Margery Lomax dead this morning." She looked at Mick, whose blissful slurping competed with her own high, breathy voice. There was disapproval in the look. "You said you were weaning him."

"I am."

Sig cast Bridget a sympathetic look and set a cup in front of Melanie. "Say," she said brightly, "you're just who I wanted to see, Mel. Can you whip out a couple of book

reviews for me? The books are piling up." She turned to
Bridget. "Thought you might do a couple too."

Melanie was not to be deterred by such a feeble red
herring. "Certainly," she told Sig. "But first I want Biddy to
tell me about Mrs. Lomax."

Bridget cast her eyes to heaven. "Okay, yes, I did find
Margery Lomax dead this morning."

"Good heavens." Melanie accepted tea and sipped it, her
cute little button nose quivering at the thought of so much
potential conversational matter. She was tiny and decep-
tively winsome, with a cajoling manner that masked iron
determination. Singlehandedly she'd founded the Palo Alto
Writers' Association, published a biannual collection of local
verse called *PoetTree*, and begun a yearly Verse Fest that
had grown from one afternoon at the park to an entire week
of workshops, open readings, and vehement potlucks. A
mediocre poet herself, Melanie was nevertheless good at
spotting and encouraging talent in others. "Did you know
Mrs. Lomax was Benji's aunt?"

"No!" Sig and Bridget spoke in unison, triggering Mick,
who drowsed at Bridget's breast. He howled briefly, but was
content to be put down and allowed to cruise through the
kitchen, holding onto walls and furniture while clutching a
piece of leftover breakfast toast.

"Really! Benji's aunt," Sig said slowly, her words coming
out in a low growl. Sig's husky voice got her more dates than
even her long, shapely legs. "Now that you mention it, I do
recall hearing about that at a party one night. If he gets Mrs.
Lomax's loot, he could put off job-hunting the rest of his life,
instead of just for the foreseeable future."

Bridget patted Sig's hand. "Now, don't be bitter. I thought
you two parted friends."

"Oh, sure," Sig sniffed. "Benji doesn't have the energy to
make anyone his enemy. He just sort of languidly disposes of
your friendship if it gets to be a lot of trouble." In her
perpetual quest for a mate, Sig had briefly gone out with Ben
MacIntyre, called Benji by everyone because of his big,

brown, lugubrious eyes. He too was part of the poets' group. He wrote long, mournful verses about struggle and toil, full of extended metaphors likening life to bicycling. The last job he'd had that anyone could remember had been a teaching assistantship at Stanford, shortly before he'd dropped out of graduate school. That was six years ago.

"There's a motive all right," Melanie said briskly. Her forceful manner was incongruous with her china-doll prettiness, but organization and accomplishment were the twin gods she worshipped. She took charge wherever she was. Now, when Bridget's teacup rattled in her shaky hands, Melanie looked at her with concern. "Poor thing, you're white as a sheet. Here, I've got something to relax you." She opened her Guatamalan bag and brought out a small cloisonné case, from which she extracted a joint.

"Hey, all right." Sig smacked her lips while Melanie lit it. "Just what we need after the shock. It isn't every day we find a body."

"What do you mean, we?" Bridget waved the joint away. "Don't light that thing! Sig, don't you remember? I'm expecting the police over any minute! Now put it out!"

"Relax," Melanie said, dragging on the joint and talking closed-mouthed, letting little dribbles of smoke out the corners of her mouth. "We'll peel an orange and no one will know. The police don't care about marijuana any more anyway. Here, have a hit."

Shrugging, Bridget opened the casement window behind her chair. She resolutely declined the joint, though. "Whatever possessed you to haul this out at nine-thirty in the morning?"

Melanie passed the joint to Sig. "Had it in the car—my emergency ration. I knew you were too uptight for coke, sweetie. Look here, mothers need their crutch too, you know."

Sig giggled and handed the joint to Bridget. "You'll go running for the shelter of your mother's little helper," she sang, off-key.

Bridget stubbed out the joint. "Listen, that's it. If Sig's going to start singing, you'll have to leave."

Melanie paid no attention to such poor-spirited talk. Like everything else she owned, her marijuana was obviously of the best quality. It had made Sig soft around the edges, but Melanie appeared unaffected. "So Benji has a motive," she said. "Who else?"

Bridget dropped the roach into Melanie's bag and closed it. "I'm sure she wasn't murdered. How could you kill somebody just by tossing them in a dumpster? But I wouldn't be surprised if one of the tenants of the old mansion put a curse on her. There was a big stink when Mrs. Lomax turned them out to tear it down. There must have been six or seven apartments in the thing. One of the last low-rent places around here. It sure caused a furor. Petitions passed, threats made in the city council—you know."

The other women nodded gloomily. Everyone in Palo Alto knew. All over town old and sometimes beautiful buildings had been torn down to make way for tall new offices and condominiums. There was so much outrage over development that the city council had taken the drastic step of halting development while they thought, a lengthy process that had ended with tighter restrictions. Unfortunately, those with building permits in the pipeline had been unaffected by the new restrictions. And Mrs. Lomax had gotten her permit well before the cut-off date.

"What's Mrs. Lomax's husband like? Isn't the husband the most likely suspect?" Sig threw the question out.

"Fred Lomax?" Melanie fielded it. She knew everything about everyone. "Nice enough guy. Has a private law practice downtown, but spends most of his time writing up contracts and such for Margery's business. I met him one night at a city council meeting." Besides being the doyenne of the local poetry scene, Melanie had grown up with half the members of the city government. "I don't think he would kill, though. I kinda had the impression he was pussy-whipped, you know?"

"Really, Mel." Signe giggled. "What a term for a neo-feminist to use."

"It's the truth." Melanie slung her bag over her shoulder and detached Mick's buttery hands from her well-pressed corduroy pants. "He was too much under Margery's thumb to blow his nose without permission." Her eyes narrowed. "So maybe he wanted out from under. I'll put my money on Fred Lomax after all. Better him than Benji."

Bridget shook her head. "What is this, a sweepstakes?" She frowned at Sig, who was doodling on her yellow pad. "Next thing you know we'll be picking the suspect of our choice for a betting pool."

"That's not a bad idea," Sig said. "I choose Benji."

"Oh, for heaven's sake!" Bridget threw her hands into the air. "A woman is dead! Someone killed her! And you guys are turning it into a game! That's—it's callous disregard for human life, that's what it is."

Sig had the grace to look a little shamefaced, but she spoke up defensively. "It would be different if it was Mother Teresa or something. But Margery Lomax!"

"Right," Melanie chimed in. "Do you remember the time she tried to put that old neighborhood grocery out of business because she said it was too tacky to be next door to her fancy new condos?"

"All right," Bridget said, "she was a slime and a weasel. But since when has that been punishable by death?"

Mick created a diversion, having edged around the table until he could grab the towel that shrouded the teapot. Sig leaped to save him.

"This kid is a menace!" She glared fondly down at Mick and swept him up for a cuddle. "When are you, my so-called friends, going to find the father of my unborn children and present him to me?"

Melanie moved toward the door. "Come to the reading Thursday. We've gotten a few new poets in the last couple of months."

"No thanks." Sig put Mick down and poured herself

another cup of tea. "Benji was poet enough for me. He spends all his energy on obsessive bicycle riding and those interminable verses of his. There's nothing left over for more hormonal activities."

Melanie hustled out, primed with fresh gossip for her day. Mick gave up cruising for crawling and headed for his big brothers' toys at a fast clip. Feeling drained of energy, Bridget sat back in the old hightop rocking chair. The doorbell rang again.

Sig leaped to answer it, hissing, "Here he is—the possible future Mr. Signe Harrison!"

This time it was Detective Drake. He blinked at Sig's enthusiastic greeting. "Mrs. Montrose?"

"In the kitchen," Bridget called. She would have stood up, but discovered that shock and Melanie's overwhelming presence had robbed her of ertia.

Drake came in looking curious, glancing around at the big, drafty casement windows, the old Wedgewood stove, the jumble of dirty dishes, play dough, kids' pictures and half-finished projects that littered every surface of the room. Bridget saw the familiar clutter briefly through his eyes and decided that today she really would clean.

"Feeling better?" His eyes flicked briefly over the ashtray, pristine except for a couple of thin curls of ash. Guiltily Bridget remembered that they hadn't peeled an orange, as Melanie had suggested.

"Fine, thanks," she replied inanely. Sig cleared her throat. "This is my friend Signe Harrison. She writes for the *Redwood Crier*."

"Detective Drake," Sig murmured modestly. "If I could have a few statements for the paper . . ." Fluttering her lashes, she pinned on her most eager, most hopeful expression.

"Later," Drake said absently. His whole attention was focused on Bridget. Such scrutiny was unnerving. "I want to take Mrs. Montrose through her statement now. Perhaps you could call me tomorrow and I'll let you know what progress we have."

Pouting, Sig took herself off. The house was quiet except for the sound of Mick's happy nonsense song from the boys' room, where he was no doubt up to his elbows in his brothers' most treasured possessions. "Just a minute," Bridget told Drake. "I have to check the baby."

Mick was sticking bristle blocks together with intense concentration, humming a tuneless string of babble. She picked him up in one arm, the blocks in the other, and plopped him down in the middle of the living room where she could see him from the kitchen table.

Detective Drake looked bemused. "Did he do those?" He pointed to a line of clay sculptures that marched along a newspaper on one countertop. "Kind of young for it, isn't he?"

"Those are Corky's," Bridget told him. "He's six. They're dinosaurs, can't you tell? The blobbier ones behind them are Sam's—he's three."

"Three boys." Lt. Drake shook his head, marvelling. "And you still have time for this." He squashed the crumbs of ash in the ashtray with an ink-stained finger.

Bridget blushed. "Wasn't my idea," she mumbled. "Mel— a friend of mine said the police weren't interested in marijuana any more. And Sig said earlier that they don't bother to detect—they just find the obvious criminal or call it quits." She looked at Detective Drake's face. He didn't look like a stereotyped policeman. His forehead was broad, his lips thin and sensitive-looking. There was some grey in the unkempt curls of his hair. She judged him to be late thirties, perhaps three or four years older than she was.

"Well, let's get down to business and you can see for yourself how well we detect. Now, Mrs. Montrose. Your full name is—"

"Bridget. What's your name?" Bridget put her hands up to her cheeks. "I didn't mean to say that. This is—I'm nervous. I've never found a body before."

"It probably is nerve-wracking," he said gravely. But he lifted an eyebrow above the wire rims. Though the glasses reflected the light, she could see for an instant that his eyes were blue-grey, and full of laughter. "It's Paul."

"Huh? I beg—oh. Paul Drake." She thought for a minute. "Paul Drake—hey, shouldn't you be a private detective?"

He sighed. "I can always tell the Perry Mason fans. Unfortunately for me, my parents were among them. Well? Was your maiden name O'Shaughnessy?"

Bridget laughed. "No, worse luck. My maiden name was Blaine. My parents were guilty of nothing worse than alliteration." She unwrapped the teapot, rummaging as an afterthought in the cupboard behind her for another cup. There were no clean cups. She rinsed out Melanie's and poured some tea into it for Paul Drake. "Did you go into police work to spite your parents?"

"Not at all. My father, as it happens, is a cop in Seattle." He studied a trace of lipstick stain on his cup before wiping it off with meticulous politeness on a snowy handkerchief that he put back in his pocket.

"That'll give your wife pause." Bridget nodded at the pocket where the lipstick-stained handerchief reposed.

"Not married. Not any more." He sipped cautiously at the tea. Once more his eyes searched the counters, the stove, the refrigerator.

Bridget heaved a gallon of milk out of the refrigerator and stored the nugget of information to relay to Sig. "A policeman's lot is not a happy one."

"Hey, I'll show you some deduction. I deduce that you're a literary type. Quotations, big vocabulary—it's a cinch." He poured milk into his tea, grimacing when the container obliged with overabundance.

"Not bad, Sherlock." Bridget raised her teacup in salute. "I do have a worthless degree in literature. But I worked in advertising—before Corky was born. Now . . ." she glanced around the kitchen, the shabby living room beyond. "Now I herd children for a living."

"And discover bodies." With a brisk nod, Paul Drake brought the conversation back where it belonged. "Tell me what happened this morning."

He listened intently when she described yet again her finding of the body. "You knew Mrs. Lomax?"

"I knew of her." Bridget hesitated. "I saw her at the city council meeting when they were approving the building permit for those condos. But we didn't move in the same circles."

"You're the second person so far to mention that meeting." Drake scratched his chin, where last night's stubble still resided. "Must have been some confrontation."

"You said it." Bridget stared at the tea leaves in the bottom of her cup. "There was a lot of feeling in the neighborhood that the mansion should be saved. But there wasn't time to get it on the Historic Register, and the city was helpless. There was no reason not to grant approval of her permit— she knew all the procedures and there were no loopholes. When they opened the meeting for public comment I thought there was going to be a riot."

Drake flipped open a little notebook. "According to my information, several threats against Mrs. Lomax were made at the meeting. A Mr. Martin Hertschorn—"

"Martin was one of the tenants," Bridget said slowly, frowning. "He has very strong views on land-use policy. But—that meeting was months ago! Why would anyone there wait until the mansion was torn down and the condos almost done? That doesn't make sense."

"I wouldn't worry about it," Drake said absently. He had taken a sheaf of papers from another pocket of his jacket and was thumbing through them. "Now, you are acquainted with a Benjamin MacIntyre? What can you tell me about his relationship with his aunt?"

"Nothing," Bridget cried. "I mean, I didn't even realize they were related until Mel—until someone mentioned it this morning. How do you know that I know Benji?"

"We have our ways," Drake said mysteriously. "If you

must know, one of the patrolmen dates a librarian who's a member of your writers' group, and he's seen you at the readings. Gave me a copy of that little booklet your group puts out—" He dragged a dogeared *PoetTree* from his outside pocket. "I read your contribution. Enjoyed it very much."

"Some deducer you are," Bridget muttered. It always embarrassed her when people referred to her poetry, which she considered mediocre and only allowed Melanie to publish because Melanie rarely asked permission before publishing it.

"Seducer?" Paul Drake looked confused. "Beg pardon?"

"Deducer, I said." Bridget glared at him. "You knew all along I had—pretensions to literature."

"I wouldn't call it pretensions," Drake said, unmoved by her glare. "In your writing group, according to the guy who gave me this—" he waggled the *PoetTree* before stuffing it back into a pocket "—a good portion of the members daylight as engineers, computer programmers—"

Bridget got up and took her cup to the sink. "Is there anything else I can do for you?"

"Hope so, Mrs. Montrose." His formal use of her name now seemed sarcastic. "Maybe you can tell me what your friend Benji does for a living. Is he one of those technical people?"

"You know everything else. Don't tell me you don't know already what Benji's job is." Bridget laughed shortly. "Good heavens, you couldn't pick a less likely suspect."

"What makes you think he's a suspect?"

"You're not the only one who can deduce." She turned to face him. "I deduce that you think Mrs. Lomax was murdered, although I don't see how stuffing someone into a dumpster could murder them."

"She was dead before then."

I knew that, Bridget thought. She stared at Drake and thought of those legs, pointing stiffly to the sky. "Rigor mortis! That's why her legs stuck up like that, I bet." She had

a brief flash of exhilaration, as if a mystery story had come
to life.

"Good deducing."

"So you can't think I did it, if she was dead long before I
got there."

He rubbed his stubbly chin again, and she noticed that his
hands were small for a man, though square and sure in their
movements. They had a refinement that was at odds with his
stocky, workmanlike body. "We never suspected you of
committing the murder. I'm sorry if I gave you that
impression."

"Oh, I probably picked it up for free." She smiled
brilliantly at him in her relief. Then her smile faded. "It
happened so close to our house. Is it—do you think it's a
loony? One of those serial killers?"

"We can't totally discount that idea, of course. But I don't
think you have anything to worry about, if you've told me
everything."

"I have nothing to hide." Bridget spoke sharply, but her
conscience nudged her. "That is—"

"You remember something else?" Paul Drake leaned forward intently. "Don't try to hide anything or shield anyone,
Bridget. It just makes a lot of confusion, and we find out in
the end."

"I'm not stupid," Bridget said huffily. "I've told you
everything I saw." It was nothing she saw that made her
uneasy. And she was under no compunction to tell the police
every bit of strange behavior by her friends. "If there's
nothing else—? I have a lot to do, as you can see." She
gestured grandly around the disheveled kitchen.

"Yes, ma'am," Drake said politely. "I will need to talk to
you again." He glanced down at a small notebook and made
a couple of notations. "Would the evening be convenient, or
would your husband object?" His voice seemed careful,
studied.

"Emery wouldn't care," Bridget said, taken aback. "But I
probably would. The evenings are hectic, and I'm pooped

by the time the kids are in bed. I'd rather come to your office while the older boys are in school."

Drake stared at her for a second longer than he needed to, the light catching his glasses so she couldn't see his eyes. "Fine. I'll call you to set up a time."

She had ushered him out before she realized that she'd wanted some information. Why had he asked so many questions about Benji? Why did she get the feeling that, despite his denial, he connected her in some way with the crime?

"I blew it, Mick," she told the baby. He threw a bristle block across the room and burst into tears. She picked him up to comfort him, but absently. "I wonder who he thinks did it."

# 4

FRED LOMAX DIDN'T appear to be grieving heavily. He was jittery, though. He bounced around the big, fancy living room like a renegade tennis ball, heedless of the dents his golf shoes made in the lush nap of the Persian carpet. They had passed his golf clubs in the hall, leaning next to the door in abandonment. Evidently Fred hadn't had time to change after hearing of his bereavement.

"I don't know what I can tell you," he said again, fingering the fringe on the heavy brocade drapes that guarded the room against any daylight intrusion. "Margery is—was—busy, every minute of the day. I don't know everything she's up to." He showed the whites of his eyes and corrected himself. "Everything she was up to."

"You didn't know she was out last night?" Bruno was talking, his voice gentle and nonthreatening, but by its very niceness demanding answers. A married couple, he seemed to be wondering, that doesn't each know how the other is spending the evening? Very strange.

"No—yes! That is, I knew she wasn't home, of course." Fred bounded over to the imposing marble-framed fireplace. The mantel was just too high for him to lean against comfortably. "She said she planned to visit the construction site. I offered to go with her, and she said it wasn't necessary."

"Did you offer because you were worried about her?"

Bruno asked the question like he really wanted to know the answer, like the answer really mattered to him.

Paul sat silent in a hideously uncomfortable Queen Anne side chair and thought that Bruno had been a fine one to warn him about getting involved with suspects. Bruno empathized with every one. He saw each person as representative of the human race, therefore inherently lovable. For anyone bereaved or in trouble, he had an even greater tenderness.

Gazing dispassionately at Fred Lomax, Paul thought it amazing that Bruno could get worked up about him. Lomax was a lot like a nervous, petulant Pekinese one of his aunts had once had. Hopping around the room with his Adam's apple bobbling in his skinny neck, never looking anyone in the eye, Fred Lomax was about as unprepossessing as any man could get.

"Not to say worried," Lomax confided to Bruno. Witnesses couldn't resist Bruno any more than he could resist them. They cheerfully told him complete autobiographies if there was time, and sometimes if there wasn't. "She has— had so much energy. Always going, always charging ahead. 'Margy,' I said to her more than once. 'Slow down. You can't work twenty-four hours a day.'" He shook his head. "Now see what it's come to. If she'd been in her room where she should have been, this would never have happened."

"You have separate bedrooms?" Bruno might be soft about the people he interviewed, but he never failed to dig for information.

"Well, she liked to work late at night, with papers scattered all over the bed—I could never get a good night's sleep." Fred's plaint had something shifty about it. "It's been years since we slept in the same room." He looked from Bruno to Paul, his watery eyes seeking reassurance. "Ann Landers recommends it."

"So you just went to bed without trying to find out where your wife was." Paul let the skepticism show in his voice.

This usually made the interviewee even more willing to confide in Bruno, seeking his sympathetic vindication.

"She said not to wait up. She said she might be late."

"When?"

"At dinner." Fred gave up on the fireplace and perched himself on the edge of a monstrously ornate Morris chair. "She said at dinner that she had a planning commission meeting and several people to see so she wouldn't be in until late. And she did go to the meeting because there were some calls on the answering machine this morning from people wanting to talk about something she said there." He shook his head mournfully. "I warned her several times about slander. She wouldn't listen, though. Just had to speak her piece . . . " He pulled himself up with an uneasy glance at Paul.

Paul made a note to get a copy of the planning commission transcript as soon as possible. Bruno began gently leading Fred Lomax over the usual territory—enemies of the deceased, those who benefitted from her death. Fred tended to shy at both questions.

"Well, of course she had enemies! I couldn't begin to name them all. Any prominent person is going to make enemies. But you're barking up the wrong tree there. It was probably those street people!" His voice rose a notch. "They sometimes sleep in the construction sites. Margy had more than one run-in with that Captain Crunch, or whatever he calls himself."

Paul and Bruno exchanged looks. The street people were pretty numerous in downtown Palo Alto. As a result they were often accused of misdemeanors by merchants and residents who didn't like finding homeless folks curled up in their doorways and raiding their fruit trees. But this was the first time someone had implied that the street people were capable of murder.

"We'll look into it," Bruno said diplomatically. "Any other enemies?"

"Don't ask me." Fred shrugged petulantly. "And as for

who benefits, I suppose you want to know about the will. I asked my secretary to bring it over, but I can tell you offhand the provisions. I'm executor and chief beneficiary. Her nephew Ben"—here Fred's lip curled ever so slightly— "could come in for a small trust fund—on the condition that he holds down a job for a year and a day." Fred laughed. "No danger of that, I'd say. For the rest of it—a few contributions to charities and her church—the usual."

"So you are the principal legatee." Paul rolled the phrases out and watched Fred Lomax's color fluctuate.

"It's only to be expected." Fred was out of the Morris chair and over by the window again. "I am—was—her husband, after all. I might also point out—my own holdings are not inconsiderable. I don't need Margy's money to get by."

The front door banged in the distance and a woman appeared in the archway leading to the hall. "I brought the will," she said, advancing across a vast, dark plain of oriental rug. She was shorter than Fred, skinnier than Fred, and with an Adam's apple only slightly less prominent. Nevertheless, the look that passed between her and her employer fairly sizzled with passion. Paul intercepted it and it jolted him back in his chair.

Fred Lomax said only, "Thank you, Miss Dart," and took the envelope she handed out. She turned to go and found herself the recipient of Paul's unwinking stare and Bruno's soft scrutiny.

"My secretary," Fred felt obliged to say. "Miss Dart. These are the policemen investigating Margy's death, Allison."

"She jumped."

Paul and Bruno looked at each other, then back to Miss Dart. She stared impassively at them, but her eyes, hot and black, kept sliding defiantly toward Fred Lomax. The dumb adoration in them was obvious.

"Now Allison," Fred Lomax said nervously. "The police have their own theories. I'm sure they're not interested—"

"Oh, but we are." Paul pushed another Queen Anne side

chair forward. "Sit right down, Miss Dart, and tell us about it. You may have an angle we haven't considered."

Miss Dart sat, but she didn't elaborate. "She jumped. It must be obvious."

"Why do you say that?" Bruno took over, bathing her in his earnest interest.

"How else could it have happened?" Miss Dart looked them over impatiently. "No one would be around at that time of night to push her. She must have wanted to commit suicide, and jumped."

Fred rushed into speech. "Now, Allison. Miss Dart. I don't think that's what happened at all. I'm sure she just fell—an accident, a tragic accident. Or she found one of the street people there and he pushed her. That's all."

Miss Dart looked at Fred and her face softened. "Perhaps an accident," she said less certainly. "But certainly not— murder. No one would have wanted to murder her."

Fred attempted a light laugh. "Well, I did inherit a good portion of her money. But as I've explained to the officers here I don't need it. I'm sure they don't suspect me of killing her."

Paul smiled blandly. "We're not accusing anyone right now, Mr. Lomax. Just trying to get the facts."

Miss Dart looked from Fred Lomax's blotchy face to Paul's faintly menacing smile. "Well, one fact you can have is that Fred couldn't have done it," she said frostily. "He was with me last night."

Fred said, pleading, "Miss Dart—Allison! Really, there's no need to suggest—you surely don't think—"

Paul ignored this. "At what time was he with you, Miss Dart? And where?"

"From about ten p.m. until early this morning," Miss Dart said without the faintest suggestion of a blush. "At my apartment."

Fred was hopping around on one foot in an agony of half-sentences. "Miss Dart—Allison! Really, officer—it isn't—I mean, you surely must understand—"

"Is this true, Mr. Lomax?" Bruno looked serious, but not censorious. "You should have told us," he added sorrowfully. "You let us think you were here all night."

"Well, I couldn't—you can see that it's very awkward!" Fred stopped by Miss Dart's chair and took her hand. "Really, Allison," he said tenderly, "you shouldn't have come out with it like that. There's no need to drag you into this."

"There's every need, Fred." Miss Dart was resolute. "We are one flesh, or soon will be. We must face these things together. And there was no point in having the least suspicion attach to you if I could prevent that."

Paul and Bruno exchanged glances again. "You verify this story of Miss Dart's?" Paul asked Fred Lomax.

"Oh certainly. Of course, it's absolutely true." Fred spoke with confidence, but his eyes wouldn't meet either of the investigators'. "Allison and I have been—seeing each other regularly for some time now. I was planning to, well, speak to Margy soon about a—um, separation . . ."

"You were going to ask for a divorce?"

"Well, of course, eventually—I mean, Allison and I . . ." He looked down at his intended and his eyes glowed. "We didn't want to wait too long."

Bruno shrugged and got to his feet. "We'll have to ask you to come to the office, sign a statement," he told Fred Lomax, including Miss Dart with a smile. "If we have any further questions we'll get back to you."

Miss Dart saw them to the door and shut it firmly after them. It was nearing five o'clock. The sun glowed dimly through the clouds that shrouded it, reminding Paul of how it had looked early that morning when he'd gotten into his car at the start of the case. He stretched and yawned. "God, I'm starving. Whaddaya say we quit for today, get started on the reports early tomorrow?"

Bruno shook his head. "We still need to see Ben MacIntyre," he said. "And I want to know where that hard hat is. If it wasn't for that being missing, I would be more inclined toward Miss Dart's viewpoint."

"Okay, we'll see Ben MacIntyre." Paul polished his glasses and headed for his battered old Morris Minor. "And we'll get someone over to poke around here for the hard hat." He sent a disparaging glance over his shoulder at the huge bulk of the house behind them. The Lomaxes lived in the Crescent Park area of Palo Alto, where the houses were large enough to include servants' quarters and garages with room for more cars than there were residents to drive them.

This particular place was not really ugly. But the yard was simply lawn, well-tended but without grace. There were no shrubs and trees to soften the harsh lines of the two-story brick psuedo-Georgian. It was a house that proclaimed money without taste, luxury without comfort.

"Just a minute," said Bruno. Paul followed his gaze to the Mercedes parked on the concrete apron in front of the garage. The license plate read MARGY 1.

"It's her car," Paul said, stupidly.

"We're dolts!" Bruno walked over to the car. "How did it get here? Mrs. Lomax sure didn't drive it from the dumpster."

"Maybe she didn't drive last night. Maybe she took a taxi."

Bruno headed back for the house to pose new questions to Fred Lomax. Paul walked around the car, careful not to touch anything. It was unlocked, the keys in the ignition. "I'm surprised it's still here," he remarked when Bruno came back out. "Mrs. Lomax wouldn't leave it like that."

"She didn't." Bruno walked around the car, too. "Fred says she always took the car, though she sometimes asked a passenger to drive for her if it was late. He said he saw it when he snuck back early this morning and assumed his wife left it out to keep from waking him up. The garage is underneath the bedrooms." He put his notebook away. "I called Neal and he'll come right out to print it."

"Some murderer, huh?" Paul shook his head. "Tidies the body away in a dumpster, brings the car back and everything."

"Not one of the street people, then," Bruno remarked. "I

followed one down the sidewalk once. He ate three candy bars in a row and threw the wrappers on the sidewalk each time, then opened a pack of cigarettes and threw the cellophane on the ground."

"No, I mean really tidy," Paul insisted, pointing inside the passenger window. "Did you notice this?"

"What?" Bruno squinted into the window, not touching the glass. "Good grief, would you look at that!"

Reposing in the cradle of the passenger seat was a yellow hard hat, its shiny surface marred by streaks of dried mud.

# 5

After Patrolman Rucker arrived they went to interview Ben MacIntyre.

The contrast between his place and his aunt's was great. He lived in an apartment in the University Park area, one of the last bastions of semi-low rents in Palo Alto. The building had a seedy look from faded paint and windows curtained with miscellaneous materials like bedsheets and beer posters. Unpronounceable names above the mailboxes bespoke the presence of graduate students from other countries. MacIntyre's apartment was marked "Manager."

There was no answer when Bruno rang the doorbell. A window beside the door was streaky with rain-splattered dust, the curtains drawn but gaping open in the middle. Shading a spot with his hand to look inside, Paul could see an abandoned moonscape of impromptu furniture—big cushions to sit on, orange crate table, piles of magazines and papers and empty beer cans and mineral water bottles everywhere. Bruno stopped leaning on the doorbell.

A man on the way to the dumpster with a bulging plastic garbage bag shouted at them. "If you look for the manager, you will not find him easily. He will never be there, especially not when something becomes broke."

Paul twisted the doorknob gently, watching the disgruntled tenant back up the stairs. The door was locked, of course, but it was a simple lock, easy to open. "Let's go in," he suggested shamelessly. "I want to see what makes ole Benji tick."

Bruno was horrified. "Paolo, we have no search warrant. What if he comes home in the middle of things?"

Paul shrugged, took a picklock out of his pocket and jiggled it around in the lock. "We bluff," he said. "Don't come in if you don't want to."

Bruno followed him into the apartment. "I'll help," he said with resignation. "We'll be fast, okay?"

The place was such a mess that it was hard to search. At least, Paul thought, pawing through a tumult of grayish-white underwear in a drawer, they didn't have to worry about leaving traces of their presence. Ben MacIntyre's apartment already looked like it had been rooted through by rhinoceroses. Rhinoceri?

Bruno called from the living room. Paul found him standing in the closet door, looking down at a small duffle bag, the kind that straps behind a bike seat. Inside it were a few little packets of white powder and a zip-lock bag full of dried greenish wads. Paul picked up the bag and opened it. "Sinsemilla," he said, inhaling deeply. "Good stuff, this. Was the duffle bag just lying around?"

"Uh-huh." Bruno opened one of the packets carefully. "I almost didn't look in it. Figured there was nothing in the closet worth searching through this thousand-year-old laundry." The floor was knee deep in dirty cycling jerseys. Bruno dipped a finger in the packet and tasted a few grains of the powder.

"The real thing, right?" Paul grinned at Bruno. "So either Benji is a cokehead or he deals for a living."

Bruno was frowning as he dropped the duffle bag back on top of the dirty clothes pile. "Must be his own stash, Paolo. A little coke, a little dope. Not enough to be dealing. Certainly not enough to support all that." He waved toward what had been intended as a dining nook. It was the only orderly area in the apartment. Instead of a table there was a workbench, with tools neatly organized. The walls were covered with bike parts—wheels, chains, even a couple of bodies. "That's expensive—imported from Italy."

Paul shrugged. "Maybe this is what's left over from a big distribution." He urged Bruno to the door. "Let's get a search warrant and come back before he gets rid of the evidence."

Ben MacIntyre didn't appear before they got the door relocked. Bruno looked around in disgust at the weedy pavement, the scraggly agapanthus with last year's seed heads still sticking up, the scruffy cedars. "How does he keep his job? This place is a wreck."

Paul made a note to talk to the owner of the apartment building, whoever that might be. "Look, I'll put in for the search warrant and clear up at the office. Want me to drop you at your car?"

"It is time to go home," Bruno admitted. "We'll get on the reports first thing tomorrow though, you hear?"

"Right, man." Paul hated reports. But this time he was eager to read through them, sift out the evidence. "Things are so nebulous right now. We need something to tie everything together." He thought of the two strands. The writers' group that Bridget belonged to was cropping up everywhere. But then, there was the unexpected passion of Fred Lomax to cope with, and Benji's expensive habit. "Let's get going," he muttered. "I need some dinner."

"What's the matter? Mrs. Montrose didn't have enough Danish for you?"

"I didn't ask," Paul said loftily. With a sort of baffled attraction, he envisioned Bridget in her house, cuddling her baby. "She appears to be dieting."

"Oh, too bad, Paolo." Bruno was consoling. "She's not right for you then, let alone that she's happily married. You don't want to get mixed up with no dieter."

"Damned straight," Paul grumbled, pulling up in front of the police parking garage. "Right now I just want to get mixed up with two triple cheese, side order of fries. See you tomorrow."

# 6

BRIDGET BURROWED DEEPER into the bedclothes. But she couldn't shut out the sounds of Emery fixing the children's breakfast; she could hear Corky's shrill protest through two doors and a pillow.

"I wanted *raisins* on my cereal! I don't want banana!" Corky was winding up for his dramatic finale. Emery's voice had the heavy patience of a father at the end of his rope.

"You asked for banana. Now eat it!"

"More orange juice!" That was Sam. He would be munching placidly through whatever was offered. Sam never quarreled with a square meal.

She groped for another pillow, and as if it had been a signal, there was a loud trumpeting from the baby's room down the hall. Mick didn't actually cry when he was ready to emerge from his crib. He simply began making a noise as big as his one-year-old body. She knew what was coming, and shrugged the pillows off, waiting for her fate. In a few minutes Emery opened the door and dumped Mick into bed with her.

"So you're not going to run today?" He frowned down at her.

"Didn't feel up to it this morning." Bridget parried Mick's enthusiastic bounces. "I feel kind of—funny. About the Dark Tower and all."

Emery's frown cleared. "I know it was ugly finding a body, but you could make a new route for yourself and not

go past there again if you don't want to. You shouldn't lay off
too long. We need to get rid of these love handles." He sat on
the bed beside her and playfully tweaked the flesh in
question.

Bridget pushed his hand away. "I don't have to jog past it
to see it. Every dream I had last night ended with those legs
sticking up—"

"Sorry, hon." Emery kissed her chastely on the forehead.
"But you'll get over it." He sighed. "I've got a lot on my mind
today too. Meeting with the venture capitalists, interviewing
that jackass of a software engineer that wants the moon and
stars and the half of my company that the V.C. don't take—
sometimes I think about a nice, nowhere job as a grunt in
some big organization."

"It's tough, I know." Bridget's commiseration was mechan-
ical. Her problems seemed much more immediate than the
ongoing struggle Emery had been engaged in since deciding
to start his own software publishing venture. One problem
was the memory of a vague remnant of dream, somewhere
between the dreams of finding Mrs. Lomax's body. She
recollected a passionate kiss, a tender smile, a shock of curly
hair, another passionate kiss . . . "Did you wake me up in the
night last night?"

Emery looked at her, and she realized she'd interrupted a
story he'd been telling her about one of his programmers
who insisted on roller-skating through the halls at work. "No
I didn't," he said, laying a hand on her forehead. "Do you
feel okay?"

"Sure." She pushed his hand away and tried to do the same
with the dream she half-remembered. Mick brought her
back to the present, grabbing at her nightgown. "Can you
give him some oatmeal? Otherwise I'll have to nurse him,
and—"

"I know. You're trying to wean him." Emery cast his eyes
to the ceiling. "I don't think you're getting anywhere, but I'll
give him breakfast anyway. At least he won't complain in

words, like Corky does. That kid gets more obnoxious every day."

"You have to let him fix his own cereal." There was a loud scream from the kitchen. "That was *my* toast!"

"What next!" Emery grabbed Mick and went to mediate. Bridget smiled and headed for the shower. She had been in charge of breakfast before Emery had bullied her into jogging in the mornings. The best thing about jogging was that Emery had taken over breakfast duty.

In the shower she began to wake up, pushing the night-mares of the previous day out of her mind. She felt up to a few bars of "Smoke Gets In Your Eyes," a song that always sounded good in bathroom acoustics.

Drying off, she looked earnestly at her foggy reflection in the full-length mirror, hoping that three weeks of jogging had made some improvement. She appeared to have gained a little in the boobs department; otherwise, no change. There were the ten pounds that she'd never lost after Mick was born, added to the twenty pounds that were the legacy of her first two pregnancies. She patted the moisture away from the swell of her hips and thought, not for the first time, about getting her tubes tied. The mention of vasectomy made Emery blench.

When she got out of the shower Emery was already chivvying Corky into his clothes. "You'll be late for school," he was saying, threat in his voice. "Miss Hartner doesn't like you to be late, does she?"

"I *hate* Miss Hartner." Corky's voice resonated with pas-sion. "I don't want to go to school."

"I do." Sam's voice was accompanied by thumps which Bridget interpreted with no trouble as a three-year-old jumping around his room with boots on. "I love school. I love Dave and Lorraine and Ellen and—"

Bridget walked into the boys' room as she finished button-ing her shirt, in time to hear Corky say, with dark emphasis, "You don't go to real school. You just go to pre-school. I go to real school."

Sam's eyes filled with tears. Emery glared at Corky. "Now look what you've done. It's okay, Sam. Your school is just as real as your brother's." He saw Bridget in the door. "What's the matter with your son? He's as mean as a wounded grizzly this morning."

Bridget gave Corky a hug. "He got off on the wrong foot, that's all." She looked down at the rigid little body in front of her. Corky was a creature of moods, without Sam's even temperament. "Let's get back on the right foot, okay?" She let him go and they did a solemn jig.

Emery watched, bemused, as Corky brushed past him to pick up his jacket. "*C'mon*, Dad. Let's *go*. I don't want to be late for school."

With Mick perched on her hip, Bridget watched them go. Sam hopped to the car on one foot, Corky stalked to it with single-minded intensity, and Emery strode after the boys, his red hair like a bright flame in the dull February morning. She sighed and hugged the baby before setting him down in front of a bin full of blocks. As usual, she had laundry to do, dishes to wash, beds to make, clothes to pick up. The grocery list on the refrigerator had spilled over onto a second page. If she didn't get busy, she wouldn't have time to shop before picking up Corky and Sam, and taking three kids to the market was a nightmare she wanted to avoid if possible.

She'd started the laundry and finished the dishes when a car pulled into her drive. Claudia Kaplan pried herself out of her Toyota station wagon. She marched up the steps, six-feet-two of massive, confident womanhood, clad this morning in a huge wool plaid cape over sweatpants.

Standing with the door open, Bridget found herself enveloped in a warm, comforting hug that totally destroyed her composure. She emerged blinking watery eyes. "Claudia! I'm so glad you came by."

Claudia swept into the living room, doffing her cape to reveal an electric pink tunic over a grey-striped knit dress over the sweatpants. She sank into the sofa and picked up

Mick, who had been pulling at the uneven hem of her dress demandingly.

"So," Claudia said, handing Mick her car keys. "Melanie phoned me last night and told me about Mrs. Lomax. Providential, I call it."

Bridget stared at the woman she considered her mentor. Claudia wrote critically acclaimed biographies that managed to achieve modest commercial success as well, no easy feat. It was in a class she'd taught through adult education that Bridget had met her and been encouraged to overcome the stunning effects of motherhood and start writing again.

"You—you think it's good that Mrs. Lomax was murdered?"

Claudia waved a massive hand. "Naturally I would prefer that she died peacefully in her bed, or retired to Bermuda, or volunteered for a space shot to a distant galaxy. But however she's gone, I say good riddance."

Bridget plopped down in the nearest chair. "You didn't see her," she muttered. "You didn't see . . ." Somehow Claudia's visit wasn't turning out as comforting as she'd hoped it would.

"It was unpleasant, I'm sure," Claudia said briskly, reaching for her hand. "But you've had three children, Biddy. You've been through the valley of the shadow. What's more, you've lived through your offspring's vomit and shit and croup attacks. You can deal with the death of a very nasty woman."

Bridget looked at her curiously. "I didn't know you knew Mrs. Lomax."

"I didn't know her," Claudia said cautiously. "But I've been having some run-ins with her over Annette Ulrich."

"Is that whose biography you're working on now?" Mick tossed Claudia's car keys across the room and clamored loudly to get down to look for them.

Claudia put him down. She leaned back, stretching her arms along the sofa, crossing one large foot over another. She was wearing the ancient soccer shoes (relics of her late husband) that she favored for working in the garden because the spikes on the soles kept her from slipping in mud or damp grass. Bridget watched in resigned fascination as gobbets of dirt flaked off the shoes and made a small black heap on the freshly-swept floor.

"Annette is fascinating," Claudia said with the enthusiasm her subjects always aroused in her. "Did you know that when John Muir wouldn't allow her to join his Alaska expedition, she disguised herself as a man and got all the way to Fairbanks before she was found out?"

"I didn't know," Bridget said. She wrenched her mind away from the futility of housework and debated for a moment if she should probe Claudia's antagonism for Mrs. Lomax. Shrugging, she decided that she didn't want to hear—might even be afraid to hear—any more about it. "Would you like some coffee or tea?"

Claudia accepted the offer of coffee, following Bridget to the kitchen, Mick holding onto her leg and squealing with delight whenever she moved. The phone rang while Bridget was setting out cups. It was Martin Hertschorn.

"Biddy! Good morning!"

"You're up early, Martin." Bridget had called him once at ten a.m. to tell him about a writer's meeting, naively assuming that all the world would be up by then, only to receive a blast of invective that had impressed her with the need to wait until evening before trying to socialize with Martin.

"So, fortunate one," Martin said jovially. "I heard you had the privilege of finding Mrs. Lomax's wretched body. Would you like to be the star attraction at the wake I'm planning for tonight?"

"No thanks," Bridget said, shuddering.

"I suppose you're right," Martin shrieked into the phone. Bridget held it slightly away from her ear. "Only the chivalrous doer of the fell deed deserves that honor."

"Martin, that's—that's really sick," Bridget protested. "We're talking about a murderer!"

"So what?" Martin's insouciance wasn't dampened. "It's going to be a hell of a good party. Sure you want to miss it?"

Claudia raised her eyebrows and Bridget covered the receiver, whispering, "Martin. He's having a wake for Mrs. Lomax."

Holding out a hand for the phone, Claudia remarked, "Uncivilized, but amusing."

Bridget gave her the receiver. She busied herself with cups and coffee, trying not to hear Claudia's zestful sallies. It seemed she was the only person who found Mrs. Lomax's murder disquieting. For everyone else it was cause for rejoicing.

Fond though she was of Claudia, it was a relief when she finished her coffee, donned her cape, and swept out the door. The house was quiet again, except for the little tune Mick hummed.

Fighting a losing battle against disorder, Bridget swept up the dirt from Claudia's shoes and started another load of laundry. She made the beds, removing about half a pound of sand from the older boys' sheets, and hung up all the towels in the bathroom. She went so far as to look at the streaky window by the table, where the boys had used their milk to fingerpaint on the glass, but rebelled against cleaning that up. If she washed one window, the rest of them would look even worse by comparison.

Instead she wandered over to the bookshelves and perused the row of paperback mysteries. If this were a book, she would be finding clues by now, well on the way to solving everything and winning the admiration of the police.

But since it was real life, she was mystified, baffled, bewildered by her strong reaction to violent death, and the utter lack of any direction in which to go. There was no enlightenment to be found in books.

Restless, she picked up the yellow legal tablet she used when writing. Emery had given her a computer for her thirty-fourth birthday, and painstakingly taught her the basics of word processing. But somehow it seemed inappropriate for writing poetry. She didn't tell him that she composed everything on the legal pad before transferring it to diskettes.

The yellow pad was also good for lists. Bridget thought of lists as domestic poetry. They were pondered, arranged just so, and often lost before they could be implemented.

Now she made a list for that day. What she needed was something big to take her mind off the futility of sleuthing around where she wasn't wanted. After all, she had no idea how to catch a murderer. Fictional sleuths weren't burdened with one-year-old sons and endless errands and laundry. Fictional sleuths could afford the time to poke their noses into the victim's past and make elaborate charts and graphs showing where everyone was at significant times.

And given the reactions of her friends, she wasn't sure she wanted Mrs. Lomax's murderer to be caught.

She shook her head to dislodge that frightening thought, and concentrated on her list. "Books back to library," she wrote. It would do no harm just to check local references for mention of Margery Lomax. "Grocery store. Cleaners. Ask Sig about job possibilities at *Crier*."

She stared at the last four words. This was something she'd been mulling over for a while. Now that she was weaning Mick, she was at loose ends. In another month he'd be walking, independent, ready for part-time day care, if she could find a way to pay for it.

"I'll get a job," she told Mick, stuffing him into his car seat in her beat-up Suburban. He lunged around trying to reach the toys his brothers had left strewn over the seat, complaining loudly all the way to the market. Once there, he was placated with a box of animal crackers while she worked her way rapidly through her list, adding a pair of cheap pantyhose from a display by the checkout counter. "A part-time job," she muttered to him, inserting him back into the car seat. With half a box full of animal crackers left, he was contented most of the way home.

"A really good job that will fulfill my intellectual needs," she said, putting away the groceries. "I need to be more than a mother."

The life she'd had before motherhood had become indistinct, something that had happened to some other person. Some days she felt that the demands of her family enveloped her in a haze of insularity so that she couldn't see the rest of the world slipping past. It was time to get free.

"Yesiree," she grunted, digging out the most chic clothes she owned. They looked more wrinkled than chic. "The job I need has a salary attached. Sleuthing does not. Ergo, I don't sleuth."

But sleuthing, though unpaid, was difficult to avoid. She put Mick in the stroller, filled the stroller bag with overdue library books, and set off for downtown. She hadn't gotten two blocks before she saw Ben MacIntyre cycling towards her, his lanky frame hunched over the handlebars.

"Bridget!" Benji stopped his bike at the curb and waited for her to come level with him. His big brown eyes looked no more lugubrious than usual, which was to say that he looked like chief mourner at a Victorian funeral. "Isn't it incredible."

"Benji, I don't—how are you feeling? I'm so sorry—"

Benji didn't bother paying attention to this. "It's amazing," he said in his monotonous voice. When he got up to read at the writer's group, the audience knew they were in for a very soothing experience. "No one even thought to tell me. I opened the paper yesterday after I got back from biking up to Skyline and there it was. Aunt Margery in a dumpster." He blinked rapidly, and she thought she detected genuine emotion in his flat brown eyes. "To think Aunt Margery is gone—just like that. She always seemed the kind of woman who would go on and on forever."

"Were you . . . close to her?" Bridget wanted to put the question delicately, but it would be wasted on Benji, who hadn't a grain of tact himself and didn't recognize it when other people used it on him.

"I don't know what you mean by close," he said vaguely. "She was my last living relative. I'm alone in the world now."

"What about your uncle?"

"Fred?" An expression of contempt crossed Benji's face. "Strictly speaking, a man who is married to your aunt is not an uncle—not by blood. Fred has no poetry in his soul." He looked indignant. "Do you know, he simply couldn't understand how important this race is to me?"

"Which race is that, Benji?" Bridget thought that in his spandex cycling clothes Benji looked like one of those skinny dogs—a whippet or a greyhound. Or maybe more like a dragonfly or something. Hunched over the handlebars he seemed all long arms and legs, topped by the bulbous white shell of his bicycle helmet.

"You know," Benji said impatiently. "The Coast and Canyons bicycle race. Over the mountains on Highway 84 to San Gregorio Beach, and back to La Honda. I've been training for months." He spun one pedal with a big foot. "Aunt Margery understood, but Fred is a philistine. In any case, we don't see much of each other. So you were the one who found Aunt Margery?"

"I saw her first," Bridget said cautiously. She didn't particularly like being the one that finds the body. Detection fiction implied that was a shaky position. "Of course, I barely knew her."

"Oh, everybody knew Margery." Benji poised himself on his bike, ready to zoom away. "Wasn't it you who gave me that petition to sign last year, asking the council not to approve her building permit? She got you pretty fired up, as I recall."

He pedalled off before Bridget could make up her mind whether the emotion she had seen in his flat brown eyes had been malice, or not.

# 7

"ISN'T IT ASTOUNDING!" The librarian ran her light pen over
the accession number on *Gorky Rises*. "I reminded Neal
right away about that poem Benji read at the last meeting."

"What poem was that?" Bridget was trying to remember
the librarian's name. She'd met her at the poetry readings
and promptly forgotten her name, as was her habit. All she
could remember now was a faint association with *Little
Women*—Meg? Beth? Amy? Jo?

"It was about the eternal wheel of life and death—how the
grave whirls around us from material to spiritual. Don't you
remember?"

"I remember nothing," Bridget muttered. Marmee?
Laurie? "I must have nodded off for a minute there."

"I wanted to," the librarian said frankly, "but I'd just had
a cup of espresso and I was wired."

"It was bad, wasn't it? Now I remember."

"The worst." The librarian finished Bridget's books and
pushed them across the counter. "All those corny bicycle
metaphors for everything—I think they ought to impose a
five-minute limit on him. He just goes on and on. But don't
you think it's suspicious? I mean, he wrote about the nobility
of death, and then his aunt died. He might even have
inherited something."

"You think so?" Bridget kicked herself mentally. She could
have asked Benji if he'd inherited. Then she remembered

55

that she wasn't going to sleuth. "Listen, I know I should know your name, but I've forgotten it."

"Louisa." The librarian smiled at Mick, who started emitting loud squawks that meant he was ready to stroll. "Louisa Arguello. Do you think Benji will come to the next reading?"

"Dunno." Louisa, of course. Bridget stuffed her library books into the stroller bag.

"Neal's coming." Louisa blushed charmingly. She was pretty, with her short curly dark hair and petite figure. And young. Bridget's thirty-four years and three children settled heavily on her back. "My fiancé is a policeman."

Both women glanced out the front door of the library, which faced the main entrance of the police department across the street. Bridget thought of Paul Drake.

"I'll be seeing you," she told the chatty Louisa, and headed out the door.

As if she'd conjured him up, Paul Drake came running down the steps across the street as soon as she'd gained the sidewalk. "Mrs. Montrose—Bridget!"

She stopped and waited. If he hadn't been a policeman, she might have pretended not to hear and walked on. But he would have caught her. It's hard to go very fast with a stroller.

"I was just going to call you." He ran his hands through the wild thicket of his hair and smiled. He looked nice smiling. "Can we go get a cup of coffee somewhere? I need some information from you."

They walked toward University Avenue, Bridget pushing Mick. Drake steered her into a coffeeshop where the elderly waitress made a fuss over Mick and gave him a high chair and a basket of crackers to crumble. Mick ravished her in return with a full ten-tooth display and a song of happy approval.

"You sure you want to do this now?" Bridget dumped all the packets of crackers out of the basket, put three melba toasts back in, and handed the basket to Mick, cutting off his roar of protest before it could get well started. "I mean, it's likely to be pretty chaotic."

"That's fine," Drake said, staring nonetheless in awe as Mick unleashed his lungs briefly before seizing the melba toasts. Evidently the animal crackers hadn't made much of a dent in his appetite. "I just want to clarify a few things."

The coffee came, and Bridget added milk to hers. "Like what?"

"Do you want a doughnut, danish, croissant?" The waitress pinched Mick's cheek. "You charmer, you."

"Well, Mick?" Gravely Bridget waited for his reply. "Oh, too late. Time's up."

"I want a bearclaw," Drake said. "What for you, Bridget?"

"Nothing, thanks." *Not true,* screamed her stomach. *You want a jelly doughnut!* She told her stomach to shut up.

"I haven't started talking yet." Drake sounded aggrieved.

"Not you. My—" She looked around for salvation. "Mick! Must you crunch the melba toast like that?"

The bearclaw arrived. Bridget tried not to look as it started to vanish, bite by bite, into Drake's mouth. Then she looked at his lips and remembered her dream again. Even chewing, his mouth looked pretty good. He stopped chewing, and she realized she was staring.

"Would you like some?"

"No, thanks." She pulled her gaze off his mouth and offered Mick a sip of water. He wanted the whole glass. There was a brief disagreement, won by Bridget at the expense of a small tidal wave that splashed over her hand and onto her white batiste blouse. She dabbed at the water with a napkin, muttering under her breath.

"You were saying?" She glanced at Paul Drake. He was staring fixedly at the wet patch on her blouse. She looked down. Through the thin batiste the outline of her bra was visible. She didn't feel it was anything very exciting, but Drake appeared to be having some trouble tearing his eyes away.

"Yoo-hoo."

"Sorry." He met her eyes. "I didn't mean to stare."

"So what were these questions of yours?"

He reached into his jacket and pulled out a rumpled sheaf of papers. "I was looking over your statement and it struck me—let me see, now, where is it . . . oh, here. You said you went through the mud to get to the dumpster, and we confirmed that. Tracks were very visible in that mud. What I need to know is, did you see any sign of anything that seemed out of place? Anything that struck you as being odd?"

Bridget summoned up a mental picture of the dumpster and its surroundings. "Aside from the body, which actually did seem incongruous—"

"So you didn't." He made a note in a little dime-store notepad whose pages were hanging on by a couple of rings.

"Is that sinister in some way?"

"Who knows?" He was reading down her statement again. "We just like a lot of nitpicky details. You said that you didn't go all the way up to the dumpster. Did you lean forward, touch anything? The body, the dumpster?"

Bridget swallowed. It was a good thing she'd told her stomach to shut up. Jelly doughnut didn't go very well with queasiness. "No," she said hoarsely. "I wasn't even close enough for that. I just—split. Have you found out—how she died? When she died?"

"I don't have the post-mortem reports yet." The words came smoothly. He stopped patting her hand.

"And if you did, you wouldn't tell me." She spoke without rancor. After all, she wasn't going to sleuth.

"Yup." He didn't elaborate. "Did you notice anything else? The ground around the dumpster? Any footprints or suspicious noises?"

"Nothing like that." Bridget stirred the cold coffee in her cup. "I just flashed on the fact that it was a pair of human legs and ran next door. I couldn't even tell you if I went back the way I came or ran straight across the mud. I know I had to put my shoes through the washer twice afterwards."

"You went straight across the mud." Drake sounded abstracted. He was still flipping through his notes. A couple of pages detached themselves from the spiral binding and floated to the tabletop. He cursed half-heartedly and stuffed them into his pocket. "Did you see her car there? A silver Mercedes with personalized license?"

"I didn't notice it," Bridget said, patting her upper lip with a napkin dipped in her ice water. The queasiness receded.

Mick pushed away the crumbled remains of the melba toasts and indicated, at half-volume, that he was ready for something more substantial. Bridget rooted in the stroller bag and came up with a zip-lock bag of cheese cubes and another of apple slices. She made a face for Mick on the highchair tray, two cheese cubes with an apple slice smile beneath them. Beaming delightedly, Mick began to eat, savoring every morsel with a connoisseur's zest.

Drake was watching her when she looked up. "My ex-wife didn't want any kids," he said wistfully.

"It's a tough decision to make." Bridget poured the last drops of coffee into her cup, more for something to do than because she wanted it. "Kids are hard enough to raise if you want them."

"I want one."

It was the same voice Corky used in the toy store, confronted with something so grandiose and expensive that he knew immediately he'd never get it. Bridget reminded herself that she was not Paul Drake's mother. Or his toy store.

"You don't have to be married these days to have a child, if you really want one," she told him. "I know a woman who craves motherhood. Maybe you two should get together and play Adam and Eve."

"What about hiring a surrogate mother to bear my child?" He leered affably across the booth. "You looking for a job?"

"Not that job," Bridget said with firmness. "I've borne enough. I'm going back to the advertising game."

"Really?" Drake reached for the coffee pot, found it empty. "Have you found a position?"

"As good as," she said confidently. Drake merely lifted an eyebrow. He was good at spotting lies. "I was on my way to talk to them," she added, to take some of the starch out of him.

"Mustn't detain you." He stuffed all his papers back into his pocket. "Oh, by the way—"

She wiped off the worst of Mick's face with a napkin. "Yes?"

"I wondered when the next meeting of your writers' group is. Thought I might drop in."

She dropped the napkin. "You don't want to do that," she said after a minute. "It will bore you to tears. And if Benji reads—well, at least you'll get a nap out of it."

"I don't think he'll put me to sleep." Paul Drake looked at her, eyes intent behind the wire-rims. "I'm hoping you'll read. I enjoyed the poem you had in *PoetTree*. You have a gift with words."

"It's nice of you to say that." Bridget didn't think it was nice at all. He was shucking her, buttering her up to betray her fellow writers. Her work was in no way outstanding.

"I really mean it."

She pulled Mick out of the high chair and tucked him into the stroller, zipping up his windbreaker and fussing over him with her head turned away. Either Drake was sincere and had no discrimination, or he was excellent with the manure shovel and totally untrustworthy. She corrected herself. No matter what, he was untrustworthy. He appeared to be targeting the writers' group as a source of potential murderers.

"You won't find any killers among us," she said, straightening to look him in the lenses. "We're all harmless folks who get together to trade phrases. Why would we interest you?"

"Maybe I write poetry myself." He tossed some money onto the table and got up, opening the door for her so she could push the stroller through. "Next Thursday, isn't it? I believe Neal Rucker mentioned it."

So he'd known all along. She smiled jauntily at him to conceal her worries. "I'll look forward to hearing *you* read, Detective Drake."

She marched off down the sidewalk, pushing the stroller as fast as she could. But not fast enough to avoid hearing him laugh.

# 8

BRIDGET WAS HALF a block from the coffee shop when she heard her name called out. Swiveling, she could see no one she knew. There was the usual mix of intent business-suited workers, smartly-garbed suburbanites, and a cluster of punks haranguing some of the down-and-out crowd at the corner bench.

"Mrs. Montrose!" One of the down-and-outers was Captain Crunch. He jumped down from the back of the bench and parted the massed congregation of street people and punkers. Both groups stared at her, their faces blank of expression.

The punks were a colorful crowd if you excepted their clothes, which were unrelieved black. The color came from various parts of their bodies, creating well-orchestrated effects. Female punks had exquisitely painted faces, and both sexes sported wonderful erections of hair. They wore it bleached into defiant cockscombs, spiked and swirled, shaved in spots and long in others, and dyed rainbow hues.

Unlike the punks, Captain Crunch and his gang of derelicts didn't bother dying or even washing their long, straggly locks. The Captain's rumpled denims and old sheepskin jacket had a dark shiny patina, as of dirt never removed. Bridget hoped he wouldn't come too close.

He halted on the sidewalk in his usual belligerent pose. She'd made his acquaintance the year before on one of her walks along San Francisquito Creek, the bums' unofficial campground. This led to an assignment from *Redwood Crier* on the plight of the street people. Captain Crunch was the acknowledged spokesman of the derelicts, many of whom were spaced-out Vietnam veterans.

The punks were younger, mostly disaffected teenagers. They interacted with the derelicts occasionally to pool information about which merchants were hassling the weirdos. Other than that, the two groups often battled verbally over who got the prime territory of the downtown street-corner benches. The punks usually claimed possession. They were much better off than the bums, since they had actual families in the background. The bums were a busy lot, scrounging food and money for booze, and looking for nice waterproof bushes and doorways to sleep in. They didn't have as much free time to stake their claim to the sunny side of the street.

"Well, it's the Captain!" Bridget said. She found Captain Crunch a little intimidating. It was probably his unmitigated scorn for the straights, as he called everyone who didn't spend their days with a bottle of wine and a joint in Elinor Cogswell Plaza. But she also admired him a little, for preferring life as a bum to the drudgery of working, and for saying so loud and clear. "What are you up to these days?"

"Being hassled for murder, lady." Captain Crunch threw out his hands. "Me! Can you feature that?" He was incredulous.

"You! Whose murder?"

"You know, Mrs. Montrose. I saw that you found the stiff."

"Mrs. Lomax." Bridget frowned. "Why would they suspect you?"

"Hey, I had a few run-ins with that Lomax bitch. Man, she was hard! Told me she was trying to get permission from the police department to use man traps in her fucking construction sites. To keep the bums out!" He thumped his chest. "I ask you! Us bums were doin' her a favor—night watchmen, you might say." He eyed her. "You was sittin' with the dick. He after you too?"

"He says not." Bridget moved the stroller a little to keep Mick quiet. "You—were you at the Dark Tower that night? Did you see anything, Captain?"

"Naw." He shrugged, but there was something speculative in his eyes. "I gotta different hangout these days. Say, Mrs. Montrose, I wanted to tell you—"

"Yes?" The Captain seemed strangely inarticulate all of a sudden.

"Well—that article you wrote. Thanks."

"You're welcome." Bridget was touched. "You liked it?"

"Not exactly." The Captain directed a mocking grin toward her, and she had to admit that if he took a few weeks to wash off the grime he might be kind of cute. "I thought it was pretty rank, actually. But all that crap about how we was all sensitive misunderstood men doomed by Vietnam to live as disaffected wanderers—well, the cops really lapped that up. Made our lives a lot easier. Today was the first time I've been hassled seriously in a while." He gave her a thumbs up. "Maybe you could turn it into a TV series or something, get us made consultants . . . "

"I'll keep it in mind," Bridget said gravely. "I'll be the producer."

"Fine," Captain Crunch said generously. "See you around the campus."

He strolled back to the corner bench, where a couple of his bum friends were trading insults with the punkers. Bridget, bemused, aimed the stroller down the street toward the offices of the *Redwood Crier.*

# 9

SIG WAS ARGUING on the phone when Bridget arrived at the *Redwood Crier*. She parked the stroller, dug down for diaper changing equipment, and whisked Mick out of the wet and into the dry before he had time to protest.

The *Crier* was a far cry from Lou Grant. As a weekly throwaway paper, its staff was heavily weighted toward advertising. Sig was one of three newswriters working under a single editor. She handled community happenings, including arts coverage. Another writer's expertise was in local politics; the third did sports. It was a lean staff, augmented by peripheral help like Melanie, who did book reviews which the editor regarded as so much filler. Bridget had done a few book reviews and a feature or two, but the pay was abysmal unless you were a staff writer, and there were no openings among the staff writers.

"That woman can talk for hours!" Sig banged down the phone. "Who cares about the screenplay she's working on? I just want the copy on the theatre renovation." She opened a filing cabinet and took out a well-worn teddy bear. "Here you go, cutie. Mr. Bodgers needs a hug."

Mick accepted the bear with enthusiasm. "I found a father for your unborn children," Bridget said. "Detective Drake wants kids."

"Is he married?"

"Not any more."

Sig beamed. "I'll ask him for a date right away."

"Well—uh . . ." Bridget realized with disgust that she was ambivalent about Sig achieving success with Drake. "There's a slight problem."

"Tell me about it over lunch." Sig opened another file drawer and took out her purse. "Wanna go to the oyster bar or the sushi place?"

"Cooked fish please," Bridget said firmly.

Mick fell asleep on the way to the oyster bar and didn't wake up even when Bridget wedged his stroller into a corner of the tiny restaurant. It was still too early for many people to be there, and the room was quiet. Sig lowered her voice when she leaned over to spread a liberal gob of garlic butter on the fresh sourdough bread. "What is this problem, now?"

Bridget told herself that a tiny bit of garlic butter wouldn't hurt her.

"We need our food fast," she informed the waiter. "Before Mr. Lungs here wakes up."

The waiter looked warily at Mick, sleeping in his stroller like a red-haired cherub. "Right. Wine, ladies?"

"Yes!" Sig and Bridget spoke in unison.

"The problem, please," Sig said, after the wine arrived, the garlic butter had been dug into again, and a small amount of contented munching was over.

"Well—" Bridget reached for another piece of bread. This was going to be hard to say. "You'll never believe this—"

"I believe it, I believe it! Please, the suspense is killing me here."

"I think Detective Drake is—well, attracted to me."

"He's what?" Sig dropped her bread. It just missed falling in her wine glass. "Well, why not?" She looked Bridget over with narrowed eyes. "After all, you've got big bazongas, and the gents go for that." She glanced mournfully down at her own chest. "I'm going to go out and buy some padded bras."

"I like to think," Bridget said with injured dignity, "that it's my scintillating wit, my sparkling personality, the charm of my manner, that has captivated him. Not my bazongas."

"You bet," the waiter said, materializing with plates

behind Bridget's shoulder. "Bazongas have nothing to do with it."

Sig stared haughtily at the waiter. "My good fellow," she said, using her best Bryn Mawr voice, "kindly replenish the bread."

"What's this?" Bridget poked at the mound on her plate. "I thought I ordered pesto salad."

"Calamari pesto salad," the waiter said with a smirk. "Comes with lots of testicles."

"Huh?"

"Tentacles, I mean."

Bridget covered the tentacle with a noodle. "I can take the rings," she told Sig, "but the tentacles always make me feel kind of ill."

"Wanna trade?" Sig had a concoction of shellfish and fettucini which looked as if a pound of butter and a quart of cream had gone into its makeup. "Puts boobs on your chest."

"No thanks." Bridget closed her eyes and put a tentacle in her mouth, washing it down with a gulp of wine. "I think you have a mammary complex."

"Don't we all," said the waiter, returning with the bread.

"Is there no private conversation in this place?" Bridget laid down her fork to glare at the waiter, a cheeky young man with a butcher's apron tied around his waist and a fedora pushed back on his head.

"No," he said simply. "We're all hanging on your every word." He pointed back to the bar, where the cooks, also cheeky young men, waved cheerfully.

Bridget returned to her salad, eating mechanically without noticing as the tentacles slipped one by one down her throat. "Go after him," she said finally, with a pleading look at Sig. "I feel paranoid imagining that he's kind of discreetly flirting with me. What if he just wants to get my guard down and squeeze incriminating evidence from me?"

"Do you have any? Incriminating evidence, I mean." Sig finished her pasta, heaved a sigh of repletion, and grabbed the rest of the wine.

"I don't think so." Bridget pushed her plate away. "He keeps asking about the writers. Maybe he's got his eye on Benji."

"He should be so blind." Sig hooted. "Benji is as capable of stuffing someone into a dumpster as a fish is of walking around on land."

"They do that, you know." The wine began to hit Bridget. She stared owlishly at Sig. "David Attenborough—"

"Screw David Attenborough. Just let me get hold of this Detective Drake of yours, and I'll take his mind off the feeble Benji."

"What if it isn't Benji?" Bridget dragged out her most irrational fear. "What if his interest in the poets is me? As a suspect, I mean. I found the body. In books—"

"Screw murder mysteries too." Sig didn't elaborate on how that could be accomplished. "You need to get your mind off of this. You're sounding morbid."

"Right." Bridget nodded decisively, not liking the way it made the room tilt. "That's why I came to see you, really. Wanted to know if there was a vacancy at the *Crier* on the advertising side."

"There's always a vacancy on the advertising side." Sig looked earnestly across the table. "You don't want to do that, Biddy. It isn't like that ivory-tower kind of advertising writing you did years ago. It's letting the advertisers walk all over you when you're trying to write the copy, and then taking the blame when the stuff they insisted on doesn't work. It's hell—that's why there's always a vacancy."

"Damn." Woozily, Bridget realized that she couldn't put her head on the table and sob in public. "What will I do? I need a job! I've got to regain my—my—whatever it is that women lose when they turn into mothers." She looked hopefully at Sig.

"Self respect?" Sig shook her head. "You're not an unwed teenager, so it can't be that. Integrity? Salary?"

"Creative power!" Bridget brought the words out triumphantly. "That's what I need."

"You ain't gonna get it in advertising," Sig said bluntly, searching her bag for her wallet. "Let's see. I had the pasta Vongolese, you had the calamari salad, we split the wine—"

"You had more of it than I did."

"Then why am I the one trying to add up the bill?" Sig scribbled numbers on the back of the bill. "Ah, the hell with it. My treat."

"Thanks, pal."

"For what? Getting you drunk in the middle of the day? Making you swallow hordes of tentacles? Persuading you to give up advertising?"

"All of the above." Mick groaned and blinked when Bridget pulled the stroller out of the corner. "Actions of a friend."

They went out, followed by the applause of the waiters and cooks.

"Remind me next time," Sig said, "not to go there until it's crowded enough to keep everyone from hearing your conversation."

"Guess I'll head home," Bridget said uncertainly. There was no point in going back to the *Crier* to talk about a job when she reeked of tentacles and chardonnay.

"What you need to do," Sig said fondly, giving her shoulders a squeeze, "is write a novel. Full of sensitive description and teeming with literary allusion."

"Actually," Bridget said, fighting hiccups, "I don't particularly like reading those novels. They put me to sleep."

"Well, then, a biography, like Claudia. She's your mentor, right?"

"I couldn't begin to compete with Claudia." Mention of Claudia brought back her misgivings of the morning. She nearly blurted them out to Sig, but that would be like broadcasting to the entire city. "Why not suggest a romance novel and have it over with?"

"Not romance." The sun made an unexpected appearance out of week-old clouds, and Sig fumbled for sunglasses. "Too hard to get published."

"Get back to work, Signe."

It was a long stroll home, or seemed like it. Bridget forgot about stopping at the cleaners. Instead she turned Signe's words over and over. Was there a novel inside Biddy Montrose, clamoring to get out?

She put Mick down to finish his nap when they got home, pulled out her legal pad and jotted down plot ideas. Every one laid there on the page, dull and lifeless. "Face it, Montrose," she muttered. "You're no novelist." She had an hour before Mick would wake up, before it would be time to pick up Corky and Sam. Turning her back on the baskets of laundry waiting to be folded and put away, she went into Emery's study. Her computer sat on a desk that Emery had meticulously cleared of his own clutter.

Touched, she saw what she hadn't noticed before: Emery had gone out of his way to make a work space for her. The software manual for a text-editing system was stacked on the desk with her dictionary and thesaurus.

She turned the computer on and sat down in front of it. To hell with outlines. She wanted to write something—something long and intense that she could lose herself in for hours. She would figure out what to call it after it was done.

# 10

THE PHONE RANG, and Paul groaned in frustration. He was eating a sandwich at his desk instead of going out for lunch— a deliciously over-full sandwich that leaked lettuce, tomatoes, and special sauce all over the napkin he'd spread to protect his reports. If he put the sandwich down to answer the phone, it would disintegrate past the point of being pick-up-able again.

He began to cram hasty bites into his mouth, glaring at the phone. The reports had interrupted his lunch; now his lunch was interrupted by the phone. The phone call would probably be interrupted by bodies popping up all over town . . . he finished the last bite and grabbed the phone. "Hghmph?"

"Detective Drake?" The woman's voice sounded uncertain.

"This is Paul Drake." A mighty swallow cleared his throat enough to speak.

"This is Signe Harrison, from the *Crier*—remember you said to call—"

"Oh, yes, Ms. Harrison." Drake couldn't summon any enthusiasm for talking to the press right now. "Why don't you call the public relations officer for your story? That number is—"

"Oh, no." Ms. Harrison sounded very firm. "That wouldn't do at all. I also wanted to, um, give you some information."

"Information?" Drake looked at the phone. "Pertaining to the case?"

"That too." Ms. Harrison, he realized, was nervous.

"Would you prefer to come to my office?"

"No. Actually, I would prefer that you come to my place after work. I can't talk here," she added in a stagey whisper.

"Certainly. My partner and I will be glad to stop by."

"Your partner?" Ms. Harrison's voice was distinctly disappointed. Paul was struck with the realization that Signe Harrison was chasing him. It seemed a little too coincidental that a couple of hours after he unburdened himself to Bridget Montrose, her friend was calling him for a date.

"Yes, we're working together on the case." He took a deep breath. "Ms. Harrison, if Mrs. Montrose is trying to fix us up together or something—"

"Whyever would you think that?" She was feigning ignorance. He knew the sound of two women scheming.

"I just have a suspicious mind, that's all. Ms. Harrison, I make it a policy not to go out with women who are involved in a case."

"Well . . . I'm not really involved in the case. But I could tell you background information on some of the people and—well, we could just get to know each other. Exchange genetic material."

"What?" Paul shook the phone. "Sorry, my phone must be going. I thought you said—"

"IQ, Rh positive or negative, AIDS test results or whatever—the kinds of things people should know about each other before they," she paused delicately, "you know."

"No, I don't know." Paul ran a hand through his hair and glared at the telephone. "Ms. Harrison. I don't think the middle of a murder investigation is a good time to engage in—whatever it is you're suggesting."

She laughed, for the first time, and he was surprised at how he liked the sound. He tried to remember what the woman who'd opened Bridget's door that morning had looked like. Skinny, he remembered. A point against her.

"I don't mean we should leap into bed or anything, Detective Drake." She hesitated again. "Bridget told me you suspect Benji or maybe even her. Well, that's just silly. I thought we could get together, I could tell you something about the writers' community, and then you'd realize they're the unlikeliest possible suspects."

"That's not such a bad idea."

"Right." She laughed again. "And then we could get to know each other. That's all."

He was tempted. She wasn't really involved in the case, except as a friend of a witness. And the information she offered could be very handy. "Well . . . "

"Come over for dinner," she urged. "I hate to cook for just me."

"What are you having?" He tried to sound casual.

"Braised short ribs of beef with homemade noodles. My father's favorite meal."

"Your father had good taste." His mouth watered already, despite the heavy presence in his stomach of large unchewed hunks of sandwich. "What can I bring?"

"Your appetite." Her voice was definitely suggestive. Had an almost Bacall-like rasp to it. He felt better and better about the evening ahead. "And a bottle of wine, if you like."

"Great. See you around six-thirty?"

"Make it six." She was rapidly moving from skinny to slender in his estimation. Maybe she was only thin because of hating to cook for one. Maybe if he encouraged her to cook for two, she could pick up a few pounds. "And thanks— Paul."

He hung up the phone and swiveled his chair to see Bruno lounging in the door, his brown eyes disapproving.

"You're getting mixed up with the witnesses, Paolo."

"She's not a witness," Paul explained. "That was Ms. Harrison—Signe. Friend of Mrs. Montrose's. Writes for the *Crier*. And claims to have some information about that circle of writers and all."

Bruno's disapproval lightened a little. "At least she's single, right?" He mulled the name over. "Signe Harrison. She's the one that reviews the plays. Lucy didn't care much for the review of her last one." Lucy Morales was active in the community theatre, although hourly expectation of her third child had limited her participation in the current production to a backstage role.

"I'll tell Signe to lay off the criticism," Paul said, smiling. He closed his eyes in anticipation. "Short ribs and homemade noodles! If she's half as good a cook as she is a talker, I'll be in heaven."

"She's got your number, that's for sure." Bruno shrugged and headed for his office, and Paul turned back to the reports. He was going through the financial investigation of the two main beneficiaries, Fred Lomax and Benjamin MacIntyre. Fred, he noted without surprise, had some heavy gambling debts dating from a spree the year before. He'd been paying interest, according to a casino informant, but was being pressed for principal. So far, he'd failed to come up with it.

Benjamin MacIntyre had no visible means of support, unless you counted his duffle bag of illicit drugs. Frowning, Paul drummed his fingers on the desk. The apartment MacIntyre managed had belonged to his aunt, and was now the property of his uncle. He had received a small stipend and free rent, but it wasn't enough to live on by any means. A closer check would have to be made on him.

Paul strolled next door to Bruno's office. "I think we should ask MacIntyre and Fred Lomax to come down here and talk to us."

Bruno looked up from his stack of reports. "Those debts don't look too good, do they? Good idea, Paolo. I'll get one of the clerks to set it up."

"Did we get the search warrant? While MacIntyre's down here would be a good time for the boys to give his place the once-over."

Bruno flipped quickly through the neat piles of paper on his desk, then picked up the phone for a consultation with the clerk. "No dice yet. Maybe he'll spill the beans when he gets here."

Paul shook his head dubiously. "Maybe. We can ask him what he uses for money. Maybe he'll even tell us."

"I sponged off my aunt, actually, if it's any of your business." MacIntyre turned his gaze from Paul to Bruno. The total opacity of his eyes made his expression hard to read. The three of them sat in the small interview room. The vinyl upholstery cracked noisily when Paul shifted to get more comfortable.

"She supported you?"

"She gave me a place to live," MacIntyre said placidly. "And if I asked her for money, she usually gave me some. Half," he added.

"Half?"

"Half of what I asked for. So I just asked for twice as much." MacIntyre shrugged and leaned back farther in his chair. He was dressed for cycling, in tight knit pants and a thick jersey with a pocket on the back. His helmet dangled from one bony hand. He crossed his ankle over his knee, revealing boniness there too. He even had cycling shoes, black leather with strange slots and spikes on the sole.

"So do you have plans to pick up your inheritance?" Paul made the suggestion. "Get a job, collect the money . . ."

"I don't think so." MacIntyre stared at them blankly. "I really don't understand Aunt Margery. She knew that bicycle racing was my job—my life, really. If only I could explain to her." He sighed. "I'll miss her. She was a fine source of cash. And I bet Fred throws me out of the apartment now. I'll have to get my own place somewhere." He looked even more mournful, if such a thing was possible. "I understand the vacancy rate is pretty low around here."

Bruno had some more questions, but MacIntyre, though he would talk without hesitation, had nothing to say. He ended up bending their ears for twenty minutes about some bicycle race he was in training for. At last even Bruno could take no more.

Finally they all stared at each other in silence. "We'd like permission to look around your place a little," Paul said, when it was obvious that MacIntyre wasn't going to volunteer the information that his closet was the modern version of Ali Baba's cave. "Your uncle is allowing us to do so at his house."

MacIntyre didn't change his expression, but he blinked rapidly, not replying. "Aunt Margery didn't live with me," he said at last. "There's nothing at my place that pertains to her death."

Paul glanced at Bruno.

"Is there something you don't want us to see?" Bruno's voice was still polite, but not so soft as before.

"Of course. Doesn't everyone have something they don't want people snooping into?" MacIntyre got up. "Do you have a search warrant?"

"As a matter of fact, yes." Paul gestured to Neal Rucker, who had given him the high sign a few minutes into the interview and was lurking around outside the room. "Patrolman Rucker will be glad to accompany you home."

"Take Henderson with you," Bruno told Neal. MacIntyre stood wooden-faced, his flat dark eyes not giving away his feelings. He walked out between the two uniforms without another word.

"He won't be too happy if they book him." Bruno gazed down the hall after the group. "Would you call him a front runner now?"

Paul stared at Benji's skinny receding back. "I don't know," he said thoughtfully. "He's so up-front. I almost expected him to say he didn't want us to search because we'd find his stash." He rubbed his neck. "I don't think he competes with Fred in the front-runner department," he decided. "No motive. Has Fred arrived yet?"

Bruno nodded. "Sitting up front and sweating, according to the clerk." He flipped through the notes on Fred. "Those casino guys can get pretty insistent when they want to be paid."

"Well, let's have Fred in and talk about it," Paul suggested.

"Fine." Bruno stretched one hand toward the phone and then stopped. "Coffee first," he muttered. Paul followed him into his office, where the walls were papered with exuberant drawings by Morales offspring. Paul gazed at one picture, which showed a flaming sun perched atop the ridgepole of an anorexic house. His thoughts turned to Signe. She hadn't sounded too bad on the phone. What kind of wine went with short ribs?

"Stop daydreaming and let's get to Fred." Bruno punched him on the arm. "You know, when you're thinking of food you look just like a dog drooling on a bone. Someday, Paolo, that stomach of yours will get you into real trouble."

"It's not the stomach that makes the trouble, Bruno my man." Paul followed him back into the interview room and dialed the clerk's desk to tell her to send Fred in. "It's the heart. It's always the heart."

Fred Lomax came in hesitantly, smelling of nerves. Under Bruno's gentle handling he regained some of his confidence, but at the first mention of the casino debts he disintegrated.

"It's—it's true," he mumbled. "I don't have a head for gambling. Margery said—"

Bruno waited patiently until Fred could look at him again. "What did she say?" Fred didn't reply, and Bruno asked again, "What did Mrs. Lomax say?"

"She—she said she'd take care of the debts. If I would never gamble again. And of course that was reasonable. I mean—I was just so relieved . . . "

"Those enforcers can be frightening," Paul murmured. Fred turned to him eagerly.

"That's just what I told her. I was—I'm not a very brave man." For a moment, Fred squared his shoulders. "Even a brave man might hesitate to take on those—those goons. I told Margery, but she . . . " His voice trailed off.

Paul and Bruno exchanged glances, and Paul took over, his voice toughening. "She didn't want to give you the money, did she? And you don't have any of your own. You lied to us the other day when you told us you were well fixed. What

happens to the income from your law office? You gamble it
away?"

Fred shrank from the hard voice, but Paul wouldn't let up.
"Your wife told you to pay the debts yourself, didn't she?
And you realized that if she were dead you'd have plenty of
money—enough to pay off the casinos and gamble in peace
for a few years. Is that why you did it?"

Fred writhed in the straight-backed chair, turning to
Bruno for sympathy. "It wasn't like that at all," he cried. "You
don't know—Margery said she would pay it. She could be
hard—God knows she could be hard. But she wouldn't have
stood by and seen them do what they threatened. She said—
if I would give it up, she would pay them. She said, if
Allison—" He stopped and glared back and forth between
his tormenters.

Paul felt satisfaction. It was no pleasure to him to be the
hard-ass during questioning, especially if it turned out the
person he interrogated was innocent. But here was something his instinct had nosed out. He wasn't about to let go
now.

"So, if you lied to us about your money, perhaps you lied
about Miss Dart as well. Your wife wouldn't have tamely
granted you a separation, would she? If you'd gotten that
divorce, what would you live on? What if your wife hadn't
cooperated?" He looked at Fred Lomax cowering miserably
in the chair. "What really happened, Mr. Lomax? Your wife
said you'd have to give up more than gambling, didn't she?
And you got angry. You wanted her out of the way—"

"No, no!" Fred's beady eyes darted this way and that.
"You—you don't understand! She didn't understand either.
But I didn't kill her! I couldn't kill her."

"Now, now, Mr. Lomax." Bruno took over, soothing,
offering a shoulder to cry on. He was distressed that his
witness was upset. "Why don't you tell us what did happen?
Then we won't make the mistake of pinning something on
you that you didn't do."

Fred faltered out the story of that last dinner with his wife.

"She said—she would replace Allison with someone more efficient. Less attractive, she meant, I guess. Margery's always been jealous of pretty women."

Paul raised his eyebrows, remembering Miss Dart's bony outline, but Bruno quelled him with a frown. "After Mrs. Lomax left, what did you do?"

"Well, of course I went right over to Allison's. On planning commission nights we always have time to spend together. When I told her—she was wonderful. Like a rock!" For a moment Fred dwelt blissfully on his love's strength. "We knew that somehow we could work it out, you see," he told them eagerly. "There was no way I could be parted from Allison. We have so much in common. She's helping me, about the gambling. We do things together—golfing, outdoor things. It helps."

"About that night," Bruno said gently.

Fred wiped his forehead with a crumpled handkerchief. "Well, I was still upset, so Allison fixed me one of her special drinks. It always relaxes me. She's very—very nurturing, you know."

"I can imagine," Bruno said, leaning forward with flattering interest. "You must have felt much better about it."

"Oh, yes." Fred nodded. "I even slept like a rock. Usually after one of these sessions with Margery I toss and turn all night." He looked down, and Paul realized, amused, that he was blushing. "Part of it is sleeping with Allison," he admitted. "Next thing I knew it was morning—later than I usually stay at Allison's. I was worried that Margery would be up before I got home. I can't think why Allison didn't remember to set the alarm. Usually she's so good about things like that. Takes care of every detail."

Paul raised his eyebrows at Bruno. They led Fred Lomax through the rest of the questions they had for him, and he regained his composure enough to demand, at the end of the interview, that they finish in Margery's study, so he could start the estate paperwork. "Getting probate is difficult enough without falling behind in filing the relevant forms," he said fussily. "When will you unseal her files?"

"Soon," Bruno promised. "We'll be over later this afternoon to finish looking around. You understand we may have to take papers away with us if they appear relevant to our investigation." Fred began to sputter, and Bruno smiled at him nicely. "Don't worry," he said. "We'll give you a receipt for anything we remove."

"Why don't you have Miss Dart meet us there," Paul added. "She can make notes of anything we find of interest."

Fred had no objection to make to this. He pattered away, leaving Paul to wait with raised eyebrows for Bruno's first comment.

All Bruno said was, "Well!"

"Is he setting her up, do you think?" Paul prowled restlessly around the interview room. "No one can really be that naive."

"I don't know, Paolo." Bruno shook his head. "I kind of thought he was telling the truth."

"Let's get over there then," Paul said. "It's about time we had a few minutes with Miss Dart."

# 11

MARGERY LOMAX had kept her home office very organized. Papers pertaining to various development projects were neatly filed; tax information was up-to-date. Paul went through the file on the Dark Tower, his fascination growing. Mrs. Lomax had bought the old Victorian she'd torn down for what amounted to peanuts, after getting it declared a fire hazard. The projected prices of the condominium units she was building ranged from $250,000 to $400,000—each. She would have made a bundle, if she'd been alive to collect it.

"Look at this," Bruno said, bringing him back from envious musings. "Boy, this lady knows how to write a threatening letter."

The letter was from Claudia Kaplan, a name Paul found vaguely familiar. It started out maligning Mrs. Lomax's thinking ability and ended with some creative wishes for the lady's future. Paul set it aside on the pile of papers they would take with them. These included begging letters from MacIntyre, with cryptic dollar amounts noted in Mrs. Lomax's handwriting at the bottom, and another threatening letter from Martin Hertschorn, much cruder than Claudia Kaplan's. Mrs. Lomax had written on the bottom of Hertschorn's letter, "Actionable?" Someone else, Fred at a guess, had scrawled a "no" beneath.

"The Annette Ulrich estate," Bruno said knowledgeably. "Lucy was reading about it in the *Crier*. Mrs. Kaplan is writing a biography of Annette Ulrich and wants her old house here in Palo Alto fixed up for a women's center or some such thing. Mrs. Lomax wanted it for the usual."

"Condominiums?"

"That's right." Bruno picked up Claudia Kaplan's letter again and frowned down at it. "The way this sounds, Mrs. Lomax must have said something bad to Mrs. Kaplan."

"I wouldn't doubt it." Paul glanced over the letter again too. "Fred mentioned that Mrs. Lomax was prone to make wild accusations. He's dug her out of a couple of slander suits."

There was a knock on the study door, and Miss Dart appeared there, prim and proper-looking even in her golf outfit, complete with plaid skirt, V-necked sweater and kiltie golf shoes. Fred Lomax loomed behind her. Paul nearly rubbed his eyes. Fred's sweater matched Allison's, and his grey plaid pants were made from the same fabric as her skirt. They probably had matching little plaid hoods on their clubs.

"Mr. Lomax has asked me to give you any help you need with the paperwork," Allison announced in frosty tones.

"We're nearly through," Bruno said ingratiatingly, pulling up another chair near the desk.

Paul walked Fred out of the room. "We'll let you know if we need you, Mr. Lomax." He shut the door neatly in Fred's disconsolate face.

Bruno was seating Allison Dart with heartwarming concern for her comfort. "We really wanted to talk to you, Miss Dart. We need your version of events on the night Mrs. Lomax was killed."

"I don't have a version," Miss Dart said, still frosty. "The truth makes quick telling. Fred came to my place after *she* had gone to the planning commission meeting. *She* had agreed to pay his gambling debts, after the usual nasty scene. Fred was upset, poor man. We had a drink and went to bed." Two red spots began to burn in her cheeks, but she kept her chin well up. "Fred was with me all night."

Paul opened his mouth but she forestalled him. "I know, because I—I didn't sleep too well. I did drop off around three or four, and overslept. We hustled around and Fred left for his house. That's it."

"You stayed there all night with Mr. Lomax?" Bruno's voice was mild, but she caught an undertone in it that made her cautious. "You see," he added, "we've talked to your neighbor."

They had indeed talked to the neighbor, who'd had nothing concrete to say except that she'd seen Fred hurrying away at 7:30 in the morning, interspersed with a lot of gossip about loose morals. Paul admired Bruno's caginess.

The red deepened in Miss Dart's cheeks, and she lost some of her assurance. "Of course I was there." Her voice sounded blustery instead of confident. "Where else would I be?"

"You might," Paul suggested, "be at the construction site, making sure Mrs. Lomax didn't carry out her threat to separate you and Fred."

"She couldn't have." Miss Dart was shaken, no doubt about it. "She might arrange to have me fired, but that wouldn't have kept Fred away. We meant to be husband and wife, no matter what she did. I told her—"

They waited expectantly, looking at Miss Dart, who had clapped a hand over her mouth, locking the barn door after the horses had bolted.

"You want to tell us about it?" Bruno's voice was sympathetic.

"All right," Miss Dart whispered. "I did go out for a little while. I went to the planning commission meeting. They always run late, and I—I thought I could catch *her* when it was over, talk to her. Fred was sound asleep—he never knew."

"And did you talk to Mrs. Lomax?"

"I saw her for a minute," Miss Dart admitted grudgingly. "She was shouting at some big, tall woman who was shouting right back. I—I told her I wanted to talk to her, and she said she'd get to me later. She actually called me a strumpet!" The ghost of a smile touched Miss Dart's mouth. "The first time I've ever heard that word used, especially directed at me."

"And that was all?"

"Wasn't it enough?" Miss Dart pulled herself together. "I waited by her car, and wouldn't let her in until I'd told her that Fred and I would be together no matter what she did. She—she just laughed. Told me that Freddy—that's what she called him when she wanted to belittle him—Freddy would do as he was told!" Miss Dart's hands clenched in her lap. "I wanted to kill her," she said quietly. "But I couldn't think of any way to bring it off without involving Fred. I went home and got into bed with him and spent a couple of hours thinking up ways to poison her, or shoot her, or stab her—" She stopped, staring at them. They stared back. "But I didn't have to, you see. She had an accident at her construction site, and now she won't bother us again."

The exultant note in her voice made Paul uneasy. But they got nothing else out of her. He made a note to check if any one saw the confrontations after the planning commission meeting while Bruno gave Miss Dart a receipt for the papers they'd sorted out.

They stood on the steps of the Lomax place, and Paul took a deep breath of the fresh, cold air. "That place gives me the heebee-jeebees," he muttered to Bruno. "Seething passions aren't in it."

Bruno checked his watch. "I want to get home early tonight," he said worriedly. "Lucy's having a lot of Braxton-Hicks contractions."

"Fine by me. Let's drop these things at the office and call it a day." Paul turned his mind to the important matter of his upcoming dinner. "How about a Bordeaux?" Bruno knew quite a bit about wine, due to a night-school class he'd taken once in wine appreciation.

"With the short ribs?" Bruno mused for a moment, then nodded. "That would be fine, Paolo. And listen—don't let your gonads get in the way of your brain, okay?"

Paul set off down the sidewalk, feeling uncommonly cheery. "What gonads?" he asked airily. "Tonight is for my taste buds only, Bruno old buddy."

# 12

"I THINK YOU should try running in the evening." Emery was stretched on the couch, his favorite after-boys'-bedtime position.

"Oh, I wouldn't have the energy for that." Bridget was curled up in "her" chair, an overstuffed monstrosity with fading upholstery that no one else could stand. She tried to gather the mental strength to do some stretching exercises before leaving for the open reading. "I've gotten pretty comfortable the past few weeks with mornings."

Emery snorted. "Of course! Then I'm the one who gets the kids breakfast, gets them dressed, and takes them to school. Too much!" His eyes closed. "I'm exhausted!"

He didn't look it. Even prone on the couch, where his red hair clashed horribly with the faded maroon slipcover, Emery radiated energy like a lamp with a fresh lightbulb.

"It wouldn't be any better if I ran in the evening," Bridget pointed out reasonably. "Then you'd have to give them dinner, do the baths, and get them to bed."

"Okay, okay." Emery's eyes were still closed, but when she got up to walk past him he grabbed her hand and pulled her on top of him. "I'll make breakfast, but from now on you'll have to get them dressed. And only if you agree to be like putty in my hands." He slid his fingers inside the waistband of her jeans.

"Your hands are cold."

"Hey, it's working." He warmed his fingers on her hips. "The love handles are melting away."

"Do you really think so?"

"I know every inch by heart." He demonstrated. "Actually, I think I miss them."

"I'm just as much woman as I ever was," she whispered saucily, giving him a big soppy kiss that was motivated in part by guilt over the salacious thoughts she occasionally had concerning Paul Drake. Fantasies, they were. Women were supposed to nurture their fantasies these days, she told herself. Even act them out secretly with their husbands.

But she didn't want to act like Emery was anyone except himself. "I've got to go now," she murmured when his arms tightened. "Reading tonight."

He moved his hands lower. "Thought you were going to do some stretches."

"I—ah . . . was."

His eyes were the pale green of an ocean wave caught against the sun. They sparkled with mischief. "Let's have a quickie," he suggested shamelessly.

"Let's."


She was late for the reading. The podium was occupied when she sidled through the door and headed for a seat in back, where Melanie and Claudia looked like Mutt and Jeff sitting together. Martin Hertschorn sat on Claudia's other side, his long, untamed hair cascading in frizzy, greying bursts down his back.

Miss Watchett from the Senior Center read in her frail voice, a eulogy to Lou Henry Hoover, whom she'd evidently known at Stanford years ago. Bridget, with a heart as soft as a week-old grape, had tears in her eyes when it was done.

Martin leaned across Claudia and Melanie as Miss Watchett sat down. "You missed a fine party," he said in the low-volume scream that passed with him for a whisper. "We did all sorts of tasteless, tacky things, like speaking ill of the dead and—"

"Spare me," Bridget muttered, scanning the crowd. "I don't want to hear about your macabre party games." So far there was no sign of Paul Drake. She had the irrational feeling that just speaking of Mrs. Lomax would materialize him.

"Did you put your name down to read?" Melanie talked under cover of the moderator introducing the next reader.

Bridget shook her head. "I haven't felt much like poetry the last week or so." She didn't mention what she did every afternoon while Mick slept, when she poured pages into her computer in the quiet womb of the study. What was taking shape was nothing like her own practical, bustling life. As if Margery Lomax's murder had unleashed powerful, deeply hidden sources, her work took on a darkness and urgency that carried her with it, moving her through the narration without giving her time to fear it.

"Who's this reading?" The man walking to the podium was in his late twenties, not at all paunchy as so many of the men in the group were, and darkly handsome. "Sig should have come."

"One of the new guys I mentioned," Melanie whispered. "Neal something."

Bridget gulped air. "He's a cop, Melanie," she hissed, just before Neal spread his paper on the podium, and looked around modestly.

"This is about the Baylands," he said, and launched a little too fast into a sonnet.

"Passable," Melanie said when it was over. "He may be a cop, but he can write." She scribbled his name in the notebook she kept for victims of the next *PoetTree*. "Incidentally, Biddy, I wanted to put in that thing you read last time—you know, with the phallic shovel in it."

"Sure," Bridget murmured. She glanced around the room again, knowing she looked for Paul Drake, unable to stop. "Insatiable," she said under her breath. After enjoying herself with her husband, she could still think about another man.

"I'm only asking for one poem," Melanie said huffily. "I

could have asked for that rain sequence, you know. Other people are flattered that I want to publish their stuff."

"Not you," Bridget told her. "I just—" She shrugged and gave up.

"There you are." Sig plopped into the seat beside Bridget. She was happily towing Paul Drake, who took in the sights from under his mop of hair like a bright-eyed, bushy-tailed squirrel. When his eyes met Bridget's they sharpened. She smiled briefly and looked at the front of the room, where Benji moved toward the podium with his lop-legged walk.

"I don't have much to read," he announced. There was a collective sigh of relief from the roomful of people. "Just a short lyric." His eyes, Bridget saw nervously, were fixed on Drake. "'On the True Meaning of Work.'" Clearing his throat, Benji plunged into his poem in the uninflected, unpunctuated monotone he kept for reading his words aloud. "'Up the long steep hill we pedaled, straining, muscles clenched in perspirant action. Is this not work? Is this not . . .'"

Bridget quit listening.

During the break, Sig pranced around with Paul Drake as if they'd been surgically attached. It made Bridget grind her teeth to watch. It wasn't that Drake was so attentive to Sig. It was just that his presence seemed to cast a sinister glow over everything.

Bridget looked around the room. Benji and Martin Hertschorn, who whispered together in one corner, would not appear so belligerent, she thought, if it weren't for Drake turning up where he had no business. Even Melanie, who advanced purposefully on Benji, looked sharp and predatory. It was as if a harsh light had been turned on, showing up everyone's faults. She wondered what it revealed of her.

"So why don't you have anything to read?" Claudia returned from the refreshment table with a cup of coffee and gazed down at Bridget majestically. Tonight she was dressed in layer upon layer of amethyst and purple drapery, so that the effect when she walked was of an ambulatory theatre stage with the curtains closed.

"Actually," Bridget said, smiling up at Claudia's composed face, "I have been writing. Just not poetry. And nothing to tell Melanie about," she added hastily.

"I have been known to carry tales," Claudia said with great dignity. "But not when discretion is important."

"Well, I'm working on a—well, I don't know exactly what it is," Bridget admitted. "It's not a poem. It's not even a short story. Whatever it is, I've got sixty-eight pages of it already."

Claudia raised one elegant eyebrow. Her age was a matter of minor mystery among the younger members of the writing group. Her first biography had appeared thirty years ago; she had over the years added steadily to her list of titles and to her reputation as a fair but intuitive chronicler of important women's lives. "It sounds intriguing. Bring it over if you want someone to read it. I'd be glad to give you my opinion."

"There's no one whose opinion I value more." Bridget patted Claudia's purple plush-covered arm and let her gaze roam the crowded room again. Melanie was talking to Benji—probably trying to pry out of him the exact terms of his aunt's will, about which rumors were flying. And Benji might know the status of the investigation, which was another matter of general curiosity. It had been a couple of days since Bridget's last conversation with Paul Drake. She hoped Melanie would dig up some information they could chew over.

Benji's attention wasn't on Melanie, however. He was watching Paul Drake. Glancing around, Bridget saw that several people in the room were watching the detective. Drake had cornered Martin Hertschorn, who made typical vehement gestures with his arms while he spoke. Martin was about the same height as the detective, and his overgrown grey-streaked beard jutted out like it always did when he got excited. The thin, reedy tones of his voice were audible even in the conversation-filled room. As Bridget watched, he broke away from Drake and strode out the door, his face dark with anger.

Drake took off his glasses to polish them, looking after Martin. Without the glasses his eyes had none of the blurriness associated with weak sight. They were sharp—too sharp. He pushed the glasses back onto his face and walked over to Benji.

"You appear very interested in Signe's young man. Is he a poet?"

Bridget blushed. "Not at all," she told Claudia. "I mean, I'm not interested in him, and he's not a poet. He's the policeman who's investigating Mrs. Lomax's death." Across the room, Drake had detached Melanie from Benji.

"He's investigating Benji?" Claudia frowned. Melanie was making her way through the crowd in their direction. Behind her, Paul Drake and Benji ambled out the far door, deep in conversation.

"I didn't find out a damned thing." Melanie stomped up to them, looking huffy. "You'll have to talk to Drake. Or maybe Sig should do it."

"Certainly Sig, if she's so hot on the guy," Bridget said. "It doesn't really concern us anyway."

"Don't make me laugh." Melanie did laugh, shortly. "Come on, admit it, Biddy. It's one of those murder mysteries come to life. You're fascinated by it."

"It's interesting, I suppose," Bridget mumbled. "But I don't have time to detect, and frankly I don't have the faintest idea who did it."

"Your policeman seems to be broadcasting his investigation evenly," Claudia observed. Drake and Benji had come back in. Benji's face, with its usual vacuum of expression, revealed nothing. "First poor Martin, who didn't make any more fuss about Margery Lomax than he did about the chemical company that dumped into Matadero Creek. And Benji. Did you think that poem of his related to getting his inheritance?"

Melanie shrugged. "I couldn't get Benji to confirm that

story that he has to hold a job for a while to get money. Maybe it's not true."

"At any rate," Claudia said thoughtfully, "if this policeman can question Benji, I imagine he'll want to question me too."

"You?" It took Bridget a moment to pick up on this. "Why would Drake question you?"

Claudia stared at her for a moment, her thoughts concealed behind her massive composure. "You remember that I told you about Annette Ulrich."

Bridget nodded, and Melanie added helpfully, "One of the first really vocal feminists in the area, wasn't she?"

"They called her crazy and warped in the early nineteen hundreds," Claudia said with undisturbed placidity. "Ten years after she died, some man got a Pulitzer for copying her views. Well, this Lomax woman had somehow acquired development rights to Annette Ulrich's estate. Thirty-four condos, I believe that's what she had in mind." Claudia paused, her eyes fixed on Paul Drake, who had found Sig again in the crowd. "It's run down, certainly. You know where it is, Melanie. Not far from your house."

"Run down is an accurate description," Melanie said dryly. "All the roof rats in town use it as a crash pad."

"There are plans afoot to create a foundation that would renovate the estate." Claudia dismissed any cavilling with a queenly wave of her hand. "Mrs. Lomax was trying to push her condos through before the foundation could move. We tangled at a couple of planning commission meetings. After one of them she—well, she made some accusations that I should have found laughable." Claudia frowned. "I was irritated, and I wrote her a letter. I'm afraid I lost my temper a bit."

"You, Claudia?" Bridget could hardly believe it. "The woman who never gets angry no matter how slow the line in the post office is?"

"I used a few phrases that I fancy described Mrs. Lomax to a T," Claudia said, inspecting the huge topaz that glinted on one sausage-like finger. "Unfortunately, I also described my hopes for her future." She watched Sig pulling Paul Drake towards them. "I wonder if Mrs. Lomax saved that letter."

"Doesn't sound good." Melanie shook her head. "Maybe Bridget can find out about it for you." She glanced at Bridget slyly. "She has coffee dates with the great detective."

"This place," Bridget said crossly, "is worse than any small town for gossip. I had coffee with him once, so he could ask me irrelevant questions about what I noticed when I found the body. He tells me nothing. And I don't want to know anything." Sig had stopped by the refreshment table. Drake was greedily eyeing the chocolate cupcakes that Bridget had put there, leftovers from a special snack at Sam's preschool.

"Oh, come on. You're not above eyeing his cute little tush, just like the rest of us." Melanie's voice was feverish, robbed of its usual briskness. Bridget stared at her. "Sig shouldn't try to keep him all to herself."

"Melanie, how inappropriate in this era of AIDS." Claudia allowed a sarcastic smile to crack the composure of her face. She and Melanie, two strong personalities, often clashed over the direction of the poets' group. "We know you're all talk, no action, but others might be misled."

Melanie flushed. "Can't even have any fun talking nowadays," she muttered rebelliously. "It's not as if verbal adultery means anything."

"Oh, now, you wouldn't like to hear Hugh talk that way." Bridget thought about it. "And I certainly require verbal fidelity from Emery—and return the same." She had a moment's guilty thought of the lust that had been in her heart, but quelled it.

Melanie tore little bits off the edge of her empty styrofoam cup with fingers that trembled. Her face was still flushed. "Yes, but you're so Dark Ages about it, Biddy. Around here it doesn't count as cheating unless you have group sex."

"Bullshit. Not in these troublous times."

"That may be true." Melanie collected the bits of styrofoam in the bottom of her cup. "But you should hear some of the stories my neighbor tells about the swap parties they used to go to up in the City." (Melanie lived in Professorville, a gracious section of Palo Alto full of big shingled houses built in the early 1900s by Stanford professors.) "Oh, well, different era. Here he comes, tush and all. Maybe we can get some news from him."

Paul Drake stopped in front of their little group, nodding politely to Melanie. "Mrs. Dixon. Mrs. Montrose." He looked at Claudia and waited for an introduction.

Bridget tried to smile while ignoring his expectant look. "Did you put your name down to read, Detective Drake?"

Melanie raised her eyebrows. "Are you a poet? I didn't realize that's why you wanted all those back issues of *PoetTree*." She caught Bridget's eyes on her and crumbled her styrofoam coffee cup.

Drake smiled easily. "Not much of a writer myself, Mrs. Dixon. But I do admire the work of your group, especially Mrs. Montrose. I wanted the back issues so I could see what else she'd written."

Bridget's insides churned, where her flattered writer's ego fought with outrage at his underhandedness. "You could have asked me," she pointed out. "Instead of snooping."

"Unfortunately, I'm a cop, and snooping comes natural. I like the poem about the dragonfly."

Disarmed in spite of herself, Bridget choked back a retort.

"We haven't met," Drake said to Claudia. "Detective Paul Drake. I'm investigating the murder of Benji's aunt."

"I imagine it will take a while to narrow the field," Claudia said, accepting the handshake Drake pressed upon her.

"And you are?"

"Claudia Kaplan." The words were said with resignation.

"Of course, the biographer." Drake must have done his homework. "I enjoyed your book about Amelia Earhart enormously. However, there is something more topical I would like to discuss with you. May I stop by your place tomorrow?"

Claudia nodded, staring at him with dislike. "I will be available after ten," she said.

Drake turned to Bridget. "Mrs. Montrose, I did find a few more points I wanted to go over with you."

"Now?" The break was almost over. People were drifting back to stand by their seats, reluctant until the last possible moment to trust their backsides to the fiendishly uncomfortable metal chairs. "The reading's not over."

"Are you reading in the second half?"

Bridget thought of claiming that she was, but something in that bland expression told her that he'd glanced at the list, which was lying on a table by the door for anyone to see.

"No, but there are some people I want to hear," she said stubbornly.

"Can you come to my office tomorrow?"

"Will I need a lawyer?" It didn't come out sounding like a joke—her voice had gotten higher. People were noticing their group. She laughed, unconvincingly.

"Of course not. Why are you so nervous about it?" He sounded genuinely curious.

"I'm not nervous. I'm just thinking about child care."

Melanie had been listening avidly, her face turning back and forth between them like a tennis spectator. "Mick can come over and play with Susana," she put in. "With Amanda in pre-school all morning, Susana gets lonely."

Reluctantly Bridget arranged times. Paul Drake strode out of the room, his inquisition evidently over for the night.

After he'd gone, she turned to Melanie. "When did he get those back issues from you?"

"Didn't I mention that he stopped by the other day?" Melanie's air of unconcern was poorly done. Bridget shook her head, staring in silent accusation. "All right, all right. He came to ask me some questions about Benji. Naturally, I clammed up."

Naturally, Bridget thought.

"Then he asked for the back issues of *PoetTree*. I was so

relieved to be quit of him I gave him an armload and pushed him out the door."

That at least sounded likely. Bridget shook her head.

"I don't like it." They moved back to their seats for the second half of the reading, and she had to lower her voice to a hiss. "He's nosing around the writers for some reason. It can't be Benji—that's just an excuse. What is he up to?"

Melanie shrugged and turned her attention to the podium. But Bridget couldn't wrench her mind back to the readers. Half an hour later, with whispered excuses to Melanie and Claudia, she edged out the door.

It was ten o'clock, too early to go to bed, too late to linger downtown. Emery was already asleep when she got home. She tiptoed around getting ready for bed, careful not to wake him. But sleep was impossible.

She went to listen at the boys' door. The varied notes of their sleep-slowed breathing made soothing music.

She wandered farther, into the quiet study. Closing the curtains, she switched on the desk light and her computer. She had arranged with Claudia to drop off her work, whatever it was, the next day. She loaded the diskette and began going over it.

# 13

"I BELIEVE THE constabulary think I did it."

Bridget stared dumbly at the soles of Martin Hertschorn's grubby Birkenstocks. He was crawling around the edges of a magnificently smooth vegetable bed (mounded in the best French Intensive method) pushing seed potatoes into the ground with hexagonal precision.

Bridget's community garden plot was catty-corner from one of Martin's. They often ran into each other in the course of the seasons, but he rarely took time from cultivation to gossip. He had started out with one garden plot when he'd first moved into the neighborhood. Though he no longer lived in the old mansion Mrs. Lomax had torn down, he'd kept his grip on the community garden. Over the years he'd managed to amass four plots, all models of horticultural care. They would have brought tears of joy to Alan Chadwick's eyes.

Bridget, whose garden was productive but no more tidy than her house, was wont to cast envious eyes on the evidence of Martin's industry. Neat beds of beet, radish, and lettuce seedlings already flourished in cold-frames made from old casement windows. Other beds waited, their prepared surfaces looking uncomfortably like a group of fresh graves.

Shivering despite the unaccustomed sunlight, Bridget turned back to her task. Equipped only with a rusty steak knife, she was hacking dead wood out of an artichoke plant.

Mick, rendered somnolent by the wind's lullaby, nodded in his stroller.

The bright, hectic weather of late February that Sig called Indian spring had arrived that morning. Filled with the need to work on her garden before the steady, soaking rains of March and April rendered the ground unplantable muck, Bridget had packed Mick into the stroller, slung her garden basket over the handle, and headed down the block. She'd hoped for solitude and the healing that came with the smell of newly-turned earth. She'd hoped to lose for a little while the apprehension that had dogged her the past few days to the point of occasional nausea, especially when she thought of Margery Lomax's skinny legs.

And instead of peaceful communion with the soil, she'd gotten Martin Hertschorn popping up from the rosemary that edged one of his plots to begin an enthusiastic resumé of Mrs. Lomax's murder. His frank delight that she'd gone to her reward—and not a moment too soon—deepened Bridget's unease.

"I might have done it, too," he squeaked cheerfully as he pushed in the last potato and began filling the holes, patting the dirt in place with care so as to restore the potatoes' final resting place to perfection. "But actually, it didn't occur to me that she was capable of anything so human as death. God, she was mean, conniving, greedy—"

"Judge not," Bridget murmured, suprising herself. She concentrated on a stubborn piece of artichoke, sawing away at it until the broad fibrous leaf parted at last from the root. Beneath it was a covey of snails, big ones. "Yechh!"

"Hey, don't squash them!" Martin came running over when he saw her pick up a snail between unwilling finger and thumb. "Those are eating size."

"You . . . eat them?"

"Of course—free protein." He squatted by the artichoke and collected the biggest snails in a cardboard milk carton he produced from a little cache at the back of his garden plot.

"I feed them on cornmeal for a few days and then—*voilà! Escargot!*"

"What's the French for slime?" Bridget forced down a tremor of queasiness. "Don't tell me!" She raised her hand when he obediently began to produce dipthongs. "I don't want to think about it." She searched for a change of topic. "So why do the police think you did it?"

Martin was perfectly happy to continue canvassing the murder of his arch-enemy. "Well, my unrepressed glee at her demise probably has something to do with it. But I'm no hypocrite. With her gone, a lot of development will come to a screeching halt. Hopefully the city will amend its land use policies before her estate can regroup." He smoothed an infinitesimal dip out of his potato bed surface.

"I guess you have an alibi?" Bridget kept her voice casual, but she was berating herself inside. Her stomach still twisted. Detection was bad for her. She should keep her nose out of it.

There was no point in suspecting Martin; anyone ruthless enough to kill a woman by pushing her out a third-story window couldn't be calmly planting potatoes a few days later.

"Not really." Martin opened the sash on one of his casement cold frames and began thinning baby lettuces, putting the thinnings frugally into a plastic bag. The delicate little leaves flaunted a pastel frilliness in his earth-stained fingers. "Just what anyone has—I was home, in bed asleep. Unless she was killed before eleven," he added reflectively. "I was listening to the radio until then."

He watched her with wide-eyed innocence. She had seen that look often enough on Sam's face after he'd wreaked catastrophe on the newly-tidied shelves of toys.

"It's all moot anyway," he added casually as Bridget gathered up her steak knife and the ancient garden fork that constituted most of her horticultural equipment.

"Oh?" She tucked the tools into her garden basket, along with two scrawny artichokes and some onions left over from last fall. A heap of expiring weeds in the middle of her plot was evidence of her nervous industry. "How come?"

"They'll never find the public benefactor who killed her." Martin beamed with satisfaction. "I've taken care of that."

Bridget stopped tying Mick's hood more snugly around his face. "What? You didn't do something stupid, did you?"

Martin wore a complacent smirk. "I've muddied the waters a little," he admitted smugly. "Nothing throws the police off more than spontaneous action." He reached into his backpack and started to pull something out, then changed his mind. Bridget caught a glimpse of white plastic, crescent shaped, before he zipped the pocket again. "Did you see it? Did you recognize it?"

Bridget shook her head. "Just some plastic doodad." She gazed at him and a cold wind blew through her. "You didn't—you aren't—"

"I wasn't there when she fell, dodo," Martin said impatiently. "But when I saw she was dead I figured I might as well make a statement. She had her bony little claws around this—" he patted the zippered pocket "—so I took it." His last words rang defiantly.

Bridget stared at him for a minute. If he was the murderer, he was the world's best actor. She couldn't see him killing Mrs. Lomax, but he was egomaniac enough to think he knew better than the police. "I don't want to hear any more about it," she said disgustedly. "But if you're smart you'll go to Drake and his partner and tell them everything you did."

Martin laughed. "No way. Whenever I think about what pure poetic justice it was for Margery Lomax to end up in a dumpster, I feel that life is worth living after all." He scowled at Bridget. "Now don't you go tattling."

Glancing around, Bridget realized they were alone in the garden. It was no time to deliver a lecture on being a responsible citizen. "It's none of my affair," she said hastily, pulling the stroller after her down the path. "If you want to make an idiot of yourself, that's your lookout."

"Right." Martin turned back to pick up his snails. "Be

delighted to invite you to sample them," he said, grinning evilly.

"Aargh!" Bridget fled.

She fumed all the way home about her bad luck in running into Martin. Now she knew at least part of his guilty secret, and she'd have to decide whether to keep it to herself during her interview with Drake that afternoon or be a fink. It was unfair. She didn't want to be put in such a position.

"I'll forget all about it," she muttered to Mick as she struggled to load paper into the big fancy letter-quality printer that Emery had liberated from his company. "I'll concentrate on my own business. I'll worry about my writing instead of a so-called murder." She finally got the paper in and the printer started. Mick sat in front of it, enthralled with its noisy chatter. He shouted one of his few words at the top of his lungs.

"BangbangbangbangBANG!"

It was deafening. She tried stuffing Kleenex into her ears while she stared at the neat stack of paper the printer disgorged. The bigger the pile grew, the more nervous she got.

"I don't know what I'm doing," she mumbled. Mick ignored her in favor of his loud new friend. "This stuff is bound to be useless."

Nevertheless, when she tore off the perforated edges and separated the pages, she was entranced by her own words. They had a force, a vitality, that she was unconscious of having imparted to them.

"I'm going to take it to Claudia," she told Mick, who had used the perforated edges to make a mummy out of himself. "She'll tell me if it's any good." Glancing at the clock, Bridget realized that she would have to hurry to drop the manuscript off at Claudia's and make her appointment with Paul Drake.

She gathered up Mick's equipment, changed him, and took him to Melanie's, resolutely refusing to linger for a chat. "I'm late," she said anxiously. "Promised Claudia I'd stop by for a minute."

Melanie herded Mick and Susana toward the playroom. Her house was in its usual immaculate state. It was a struggle for Bridget to avoid comparing the neat rooms full of well-polished furniture with her own disheveled domain. "Don't hurry back," Melanie said over her shoulder. "I'll give him some lunch and then we'll go to the park. Take your time."

Claudia lived near Melanie, although her big old shingled bungalow was a polar opposite from Melanie's trimly-kept Monterey Colonial. There was no answer at the door, but Claudia's car was in the drive, so Bridget made her way through an ivy-shrouded moon gate to check the back yard.

The back of the house was a surprise after the dark ivied jungle of the front yard. Horticulture was Claudia's hobby, and roses her specialty. The sun poured down into a central grass plot, where an old sundial proclaimed the time, indifferent to the approach of daylight savings. Against the back of the house were starkly-pruned tea roses. Around the edges of the yard, almost covering an ancient greenhouse, were climbing roses. One early variety bloomed already, spilling fragrance into the tender spring air.

Bridget could hear Claudia's voice coming from the greenhouse. Clutching her manuscript in her arms, she ducked in through the low door. Inside, shadowed by the vines that reached across the top panes of glass, the greenhouse was full of gentle, diffuse light.

At each side wide planks on sawhorses supported a collection of scrounged containers with seedlings in various stages of development. More flats jostled for space on the floor down the middle of the aisle. At the end, in front of a low cabinet, padlocked doors hanging open, was Claudia. She held a large brown bottle adorned with a conspicuous skull and crossbones. Paul Drake stood in front of her, his back to Bridget, his legs belligerently straddling a flat of baby carrots.

Claudia saw Bridget and gave her a wry salute with the brown bottle. "As I was saying, Detective Drake," she remarked, her deep voice sounding calm and faintly amused, "if I had set out to murder Mrs. Lomax, I would have chosen to do it via a household accident. Arsenic in the soup, aldecarb in the peaches—if I were of a bloodthirsty turn of mind, nothing would have been easier." She turned with a gracious inclination of her head and Bridget saw Drake's partner, partially obscured in Claudia's shadow, scribbling in a notepad. "But as it happens, I rid myself of my spleen through my pen. Having annihilated Mrs. Lomax with words, I had no need to murder her in actual fact."

Drake had turned when Claudia acknowledged Bridget's presence, raking her with an absent-minded look and immediately swiveling back to Claudia. "In your letter to her," he said mildly, "you expressed a great deal of hostility and you sounded pretty active about it."

Claudia waggled the brown bottle at him with ponderous playfulness. "Detective Drake, of one thing you can be perfectly sure. If I had chosen to eliminate Mrs. Lomax, I would have done it far too cleverly for you to have found out about." She smiled with calm certainty on Drake and Morales. "A murder of my committing would never be discovered."

Sighing, Bridget leaned against the greenhouse door. Something told her it would be a while before Claudia was free to look at her manuscript.

# 14

THE SIGHT OF Bridget standing in the greenhouse door should have made Paul feel better. She looked nice, with the sun picking out red lights in her soft brown hair, her exuberant curves unquenched by the big sweater she wore. But nothing could make Paul feel better at that point.

It was nearly a week now since the murder, and they still hadn't really gotten a grip on the case. He was beginning to wonder if they'd ever find Mrs. Lomax's murderer.

Because that was one thing they definitely had pinned down. Mrs. Lomax had been murdered. One of the stray bits of two-by-four that littered the ground around the dumpster had turned out to have a few of the victim's sparse grey hairs on it. Its contours exactly fit one of the craters in Mrs. Lomax's head, where minute grains of sawdust had been found. Those committing suicide or falling by accident didn't normally hit themselves over the head first.

Someone had hit her, pushed her out the window, tossed the improvised club after her. And up to now that someone had gotten off scot-free.

The days that Paul and Bruno had spent doggedly following up every nuance of every clue had gotten them nowhere. They were still running down alleys, hoping each time that one of them wouldn't be blind.

Miss Dart had been looking good, but they had no evidence to place her at the construction site. In fact, a couple of lingering planning commissioners had seen her neat subcompact going off in the opposite direction from Mrs. Lomax's Mercedes. With Fred and Allison willing to swear to each other's whereabouts it seemed pretty hopeless to pin anything on them, unless an undiscovered clue came out.

As principal legatee, Fred still retained his place high on the suspect list. But much of Mrs. Lomax's money had been tied up in her company, and Lomax Development stood to lose money, since several construction projects were held in abeyance until probate closed. At the last interview in what had been her office, Fred's harassed plaint of slipping schedules, cost overruns, and idle work crews made it obvious that without the hard-nosed genius of its founding mother, Lomax Development was liable to go down the tubes.

Then the promising avenue of MacIntyre's closet stash had also turned into a blind alley. Though they'd turned his place upside down, Rucker and Henderson had found no little white packets, no zip-lock bags of sinsemilla. All they'd found was a small amount of hashish and a lot of imported bicycle equipment that didn't look as if it had come through customs.

MacIntyre had had time to dispose of the contents of his duffle bag—but why had he done so? Had he gotten a tip? That thought made Paul profoundly uneasy. And if he knew a search was coming, why hadn't he gotten rid of the hashish? According to the search team, he'd resented like hell that they appropriated the stuff, no matter that it was illegal. If he was a drug dealer, he seemed like a singularly inept one.

Paul had had one unsatisfactory talk with Martin Hertschorn at the writers' meeting the night before. Hertschorn was hard to get hold of, and had proved evasive enough to arouse some suspicion. Paul made a note to tackle Hertschorn again and pin down his alibi.

The night before he'd met Bruno at a downtown bar after leaving the poetry reading. Sometimes these sessions, away from the pressures of the office, produced valuable insights and relevations. Last night had produced only a beer that he didn't really want and a headache.

He had grumbled to Bruno that they didn't have the experience to solve a murder case like this. "That guy getting his head kicked in on University Avenue—that time there were witnesses and motives galore. That was easy." He drained the beer and shook his head when the waitress swooped by for the glass. "This one—who knows why she was murdered? It could even have been one of the street people that old Fred keeps harping on. I don't know. I never felt less like Sam Spade."

Bruno listened with half an ear. He had his own preoccupations. Lucy Morales was too pregnant for him to feel comfortable away from her at night. "The third one—it's going to come so fast," he predicted, his brown eyes worried. "The second one—hell, we were only at the hospital for half an hour when he popped out. With this one we may not make it to the car!"

Little X Morales, as the clerks at work were calling it, was taking its time appearing, which made Bruno a jittery partner to work with. He'd spent the morning hovering over the telephone, until Paul had dragged him away to Mrs. Kaplan's house.

With the instinct cops cultivated, they knew Mrs. Kaplan was hiding something. Though more than a little intimidated by her imposing presence, and his knowledge of her imposing reputation, Paul kept at her. Each evasive answer made Bruno's nose practically quiver. He exchanged a look of satisfaction with Paul when she finally began to talk. Her speech about murder was interesting. A belief that they were invincible was common among murderers. Paul was intrigued to find it in one of Mrs. Lomax's enemies.

But Bridget's entrance broke the mood. Mrs. Kaplan was through making speeches. She asked if there were any more questions, shepherding them out of the greenhouse and into her dilapidated kitchen, magnificently unconcerned about the little blobs of leaf mold her soccer shoes left all over the floor.

"I do have a schedule, and there's no point wasting time in gossip."

"Perhaps it's a bad time for me to burden you—" Bridget began. Paul noticed for the first time that she clutched a pile of computer paper.

"Nonsense. I particularly want to see what you've done." Mrs. Kaplan pried the bundle out of Bridget's arms. "I can give you a cup of coffee, but then I want to get started reading." She put the manuscript on a teetering pile of file folders, magazines, other manuscripts, and bulky manila envelopes. The pile gave a last shudder and tilted toward the floor. Paul and Bridget leapt to save it and ran into each other. Papers cascaded over them.

Mrs. Kaplan filled a battered teakettle, watching impassively. "Entertaining," she said. "Don't you agree, Detective Morales?"

Bruno, lips twitching, nodded his head. While Mrs. Kaplan set out cups on the linoleum counter and methodically measured coffee crystals into each one, Bruno knelt to help pick up the papers. Bridget, Paul noticed, was very solicitous of her manuscript. She gathered the pages together hastily, thumbing through to see that everything was in order. His curiosity was aroused. From the look of the pages, it wasn't poetry. He forced the topic from his mind, stacking the last envelopes and accepting a chipped mug from Mrs. Kaplan.

"I'm not sure I buy it, if you'll pardon me, Mrs. Kaplan." He kept his voice flat, unfriendly. Bridget was looking at him in surprise. "We know about the letter you wrote—Mrs. Lomax saved it. We know you made a scene after the planning commission meeting—there were plenty of people around taking in the excitement." He pulled out a notebook and thumbed carefully through it, cramming loose pages back in as they fell out. "You said, and I quote: 'You'll regret this as long as you live, Mrs. Lomax. I just hope for your sake that isn't long.'"

Bridget—incredulous concern on her face—transferred her gaze to Mrs. Kaplan. Paul tucked away his notebook containing the quote he'd read.

Mrs. Kaplan sat quite still, as if considering the weight of the damage. At last she seemed to make up her mind.

"I wasn't going to tell this to anyone," she said, going over to the pile of folders and papers. She hunted through them, adroitly managing to extract the one she wanted without upsetting the others all over the floor again. "Margery Lomax said some very unpleasant things to me at that first meeting. Among other comments, she implied that, like Annette Ulrich, I too was a lesbian." Claudia paused, looking thoughtful. "I don't really know why that stung so much. After all, it's nobody's business but mine. However it may be, I wanted to make her smart for that and for her impertinence in trying to condo-ize Annette's place."

She put both palms on the folder and leaned forward. "But the revenge I had in mind for Mrs. Lomax did not include killing her. Or at least," she added, ruminating, "not out-right." She opened the folder and looked around the table as if she were running a seminar. Paul almost got his notebook out again. "I was just going to embarrass her to death."

Paul frowned at Mrs. Kaplan, then down at the open folder. On the title page was neatly typed: MOLL FLOMAX, MEMOIRS OF A WOMAN OF REAL ESTATE. AS TOLD TO HER BIOGRAPHER, C.K.

He stared at the words, uncomprehending, and Mrs. Kaplan began to explain. "I admit it's a bit juvenile to make Margery Lomax the dubious heroine of a lascivious book. But I couldn't resist. Aside from mortifying her, it would show her that I certainly knew my way around heterosexual copulation. There's just enough truth to make her squirm," she added with relish, "not enough to be libelous. I planned to publish it myself."

Paul transferred his puzzled stare to her face. "I still don't understand. Do you think this would have succeeded in stopping Mrs. Lomax's development?"

The exasperating woman just grinned at him. "It might have made a successful bargaining chip. If she wouldn't cooperate after she saw the galleys—well, I have connections for getting distribution. With the extreme—uh, juiciness of the details—the ritualistic closing ceremonies, where loans were celebrated with the utmost license; the extra services thrown in to convince the client to buy a house—it would have been very entertaining and extremely sexy. Maybe even profitable." Mrs. Kaplan closed the file folder with a faint sigh of regret. "I was looking forward to finishing it, but now—I suppose it would be in bad taste."

Paul shut his mouth with a snap. "You know that amounts to blackmail, Mrs. Kaplan."

"We'd better take it along for evidence," Bruno put in, eyeing the folder with interest.

"If you wish." Mrs. Kaplan pushed the folder across to him. "I hadn't gotten to the really steamy parts yet, of course."

"Of course." Bruno's face fell, but he tucked the folder carefully into his briefcase. "We'll get on it right away, Mrs. Kaplan."

Paul gave up on Mrs. Kaplan and turned to Bridget. "Didn't you have an appointment with us?" He glanced at his watch. "You're late."

"So are you," Bridget pointed out. "What did you want to know, anyway?"

Mrs. Kaplan rose with dignity. "You're welcome to stay here for your interrogation, but I must excuse myself. Bridget, I'll get back to you soon." She nodded all around, swept up Bridget's manuscript, and left the room.

Paul blinked. "God save the queen," he murmured. "Bridget, I don't think you've met Bruno Morales, my partner."

Bridget smiled at Bruno. "What was it you two wanted to talk to me about?" She glanced around at Mrs. Kaplan's cluttered kitchen. "Is it okay to stay here?"

"It's fine." Paul leaned back in his chair, refusing to take another sip of his cooling coffee. Bruno, he noticed sourly, had lapped up the murky brew with enthusiasm.

"Well, Mrs. Montrose," Bruno began confidingly. Bridget began to soften up under the well-known Morales charm. "We have been talking it over, Paolo and I, and we both have the sense that something in the crime ties it to your writers' circle."

"Impossible!" Bridget sipped her coffee and choked. "None of us are violent. You just saw Claudia's method for annihilation. The pen is mightier than the sword and all that."

"The sword might look good to those of you who felt threatened by Mrs. Lomax," Paul pointed out. Bridget's distress worried and confused him. Despite the agreeable evenings he'd been spending with Signe, he still found Bridget's zaftig curves and straightforward eyes appealing. "Your friend Benji was at her mercy as far as living and eating went," he went on, the concern he felt materializing in his voice as anger. "Your friend Mrs. Kaplan wrote threatening letters and engaged in a verbal battle with the victim a few hours before her death. Your friend Martin had a big grudge against her." Bridget's eyes slid sideways, and the red color washed up her neck and over her face. Silently Paul noted it. Something there they'd have to probe for later. "And to top it all off, Mrs. Lomax owned the building your poetry readings take place in. According to her files, she was getting ready to tear it down for office condos."

That surprised her. "You must be wrong." Bridget twisted her hands together in her lap. "The community college owns that building."

"Rents it," Paul corrected. "The lease expires in June." He drew a finger graphically across his throat. "No more community college. They'll have to move."

Bruno frowned, startled by his hostility, and Paul reined himself in. "Sorry, Mrs. Montrose," he said gruffly. "At any rate, things link up. We are investigating other avenues, but we can't neglect the poets' group."

Bruno took the conversation into his own hands. "You can

see how useful we would find any background information you might be able to offer us."

Bridget kept her eyes on the black depths of her coffee mug. "Hasn't Sig told you enough?"

"She has been helpful," Paul admitted stiffly, "but strictly informally. We haven't asked her to officially assist the police."

"Official stool pigeon," Bridget mumbled to the cup. Paul barely caught her words.

"Now, Mrs. Montrose." Bruno spoke soothingly. "We aren't asking you to act as an informer or anything of that nature." He shot a reproachful glance at Paul. "We just want you to try and remember anything about anyone's behavior that's seemed unusual to you. You're a writer, an observer of people. We just want to know what, if anything, you've seen."

Paul could tell that for once Bruno's persuasive powers were going to fail. Bridget shook her head stubbornly and got to her feet.

"I have about a million children to keep track of. I don't have time to notice anything. If you'll excuse me—" She marched over to the back door and held it open. Without quite knowing how it happened, they found themselves on the steps. The door shut firmly behind them.

They walked around the side of the house, through the moon gate and the overgrown front yard. "So she won't play." Paul stopped beside his car and began to polish his wire-rims. "Told you so."

"Why did you get her back up like that?" Bruno made a couple more notes and then tucked his notebook into his briefcase. "You might have known she'd dig in her heels. And I had hopes that she could tell us something about Martin Hertschorn."

"Signe said she wouldn't cooperate." Paul sighed.

"Why doesn't your Signe have the information we want?"

"She doesn't hang out that much with the poets. She's good friends with Bridget, so she knows them all, but just general stuff, like Mrs. Kaplan's literary reputation, Benji's sluggishness, Hertschorn's resentment. None of the details."

"And you think Mrs. Montrose knows the details?" They got into the car. Paul thought about the cigarettes he'd given up four months ago. He wanted one with the kind of desperate longing that only came over him at times of extreme frustration.

"Probably she knows nothing important," he admitted. "But she's the type of woman that people tell things to, you know? And she would tell the truth, too, if she talked. Too bad she won't gossip."

"At least not with the police," Bruno acknowledged. "Well, I guess this leaves what's-her-name—the one who started the group. You know, Melanie whoever."

"Dixon." Paul started the car. "We'll drop in on her now. I got a feeling last night that she knows everything there is to know." He sighed. "Trouble is, I don't trust her not to bend the truth if it suits her. Now Bridget would never do that."

"You might have got Mrs. Montrose to cooperate if you'd approached her right. Maybe you should have asked your Signe to talk her into it."

"I did." Paul frowned. "Sig wouldn't do it. Said it wouldn't be honorable." He stuck the key in the ignition, jiggling it just so. Obediently the engine started. He figured he might as well enliven the drive to Melanie Dixon's house with a good argument, so he tossed Bruno some fighting words. "Who's she kidding? Women aren't really capable of honor at the best of times." The words came out with an unexpected bitterness when he thought of his ex-wife, whose strange sense of honor had allowed her to sleep with her aerobics instructor and lie about it, "because I didn't want to hurt you, Paul." He shook his head, ignoring Bruno's splutter of protest. "Nope," he said, "you can't expect honor from women."

# 15

CLAUDIA CAME BACK into the kitchen with suspicious promptness as soon as the policemen were gone. "What did they want to talk to you about?" She put the kettle on the stove again and regarded Bridget expectantly.

"Same old stuff." Bridget tried to put nonchalance into her shrug. Her conversation with Paul and Bruno had disturbed her, with the knowledge of Martin's secret perfidy burning a hole in her mind. She should have told them what he'd shown her that morning. But if she'd done that, it would have made her just what she'd refused to be—a stoolie, an informer.

"Like what?" Claudia sat down across from Bridget at the table. Preoccupied with her own thoughts, Bridget barely noticed.

"Wanting to know what I know about everything, I guess." It was a murder case, she argued with herself. In a murder case, there was no stigma attached to being an informer. "I've got half a mind . . . "

"I can see that." The exasperation in Claudia's voice finally jolted her out of her fog. "Half a mind to do what?"

"To call them up—tell them . . . " She stared across the table. "Claudia, if you knew something, and it implicated somebody who you were sure couldn't be the murderer, would you tell the police?"

"Of course." Claudia answered with no hesitation. "You can't conceal evidence in a murder investigation, Biddy.

Who's it about?" A shadow of uneasiness crossed her face. "Me?"

"You? Heavens, no." Bridget laughed, but her laughter died after one look at Claudia's expression. She looked— guilty. And scared. "Claudia, what is it?"

"I shouldn't have let them interview me here." Claudia twisted her hands together, ignoring the kettle when it began an insistent whine. Bridget got up and turned it off, fixing Claudia a cup of the instant coffee she lived on. "It was stupid. I was stupid. I said things—let him goad me—" She bowed her head and looked at her hands. "That Drake really pushed me—made me mad."

"Claudia, you have nothing to worry about. You're innocent." Bridget put the coffee on the table and sat beside Claudia, patting her arm. But she couldn't stop her imagination from conjuring up a picture of Claudia reaching out to push Margery Lomax, watching her fall . . . Mrs. Lomax had been tiny. Claudia was at least as strong as an average man. Bridget had seen her hoisting bags of steer manure as if they weighed nothing.

"It's so easy for them to put it together," Claudia murmured, still regarding her clasped hands. "Motive, opportunity—"

"Surely you have an alibi!"

"I was here alone, working on that ridiculous thing I gave the police," Claudia said, raising her head and finding the coffee. She sipped it, but her composure did not return. "Why did I give it to them? Just hammering another nail in their air-tight case."

"Don't be absurd." Bridget spoke stoutly, but she couldn't get that picture out of her mind.

"I've heard they can get fingerprints off of anything these days," Claudia muttered. She looked at Bridget and her gaze sharpened. "Did you say you had evidence against someone else? Who? Who is it?"

"Well—I was talking to Martin this morning," Bridget began, slightly taken aback by Claudia's vehemence. "He—

let something slip. But he asked me not to tell, so I haven't, yet."

"You should. You must." Claudia gripped her hands together again. "Martin—he'd make a good suspect. Him with his constant campaigns against development and growth. Who knows what he'd do to stop a building?"

"You're suggesting Martin in the role of sacrificial lamb?" Bridget kept her voice steady.

Claudia had the grace to look shamefaced. "I'm in a twitchet over this whole thing," she admitted. "I'm acting like a fool. Forget what I said." She took her coffee cup over to the sink.

"Maybe I shouldn't impose my manuscript on you," Bridget began, watching those trembling hands with dismay.

"Don't be absurd. I'm dying to see what you've been up to." Claudia turned from the sink, her face wearing its normal placid expression. "But Biddy—"

Bridget paused by the door. "What is it?"

"Think about what I said. Not to take the heat off of me, or anything. But whatever you know, you should tell the police." Claudia regarded her intently enough to bring goose bumps to her arms. "It's not safe for you to carry around secrets. Tell them. Let them take it from there."

"I—I'll think about it," Bridget said, shaken. "Thanks, Claudia."

# 16

As PAUL HAD known he would, Bruno took exception to his inflammatory remark about honor among women, and they argued it vigorously all the way to Melanie's house. Bruno was an unquenchable debater, always popping up with a riposte, and the issue wasn't settled to his satisfaction when they pulled up in front of Melanie Dixon's house.

Paul thought of Mrs. Dixon primarily as Bridget's friend, but he hadn't been in her house more than a minute before she began to be elevated into the ranks of those whose actions needed scrutiny. She was nervous—far too nervous for an innocent person to be at the unexpected presence of the police.

"Oh, I thought you were Biddy," she exclaimed when she opened the door. Without waiting for an invitation Paul moved into the living room, Bruno right behind him.

"Are you expecting Mrs. Montrose?"

"Not right away—well, maybe—I don't know." Melanie gave way before them, gesturing feebly toward the elegant grouping of furniture in front of one long, arched window. The room spoke of graciousness and furniture polish. From the kitchen came the loud babble of baby voices. "Isn't she supposed to be at your office? I mean, Mick's here, and I thought—"

"We just talked to Mrs. Montrose," Bruno interjected smoothly. "Can you sit down, or should we go into the kitchen? Are the kids having lunch?"

Bruno's interest appeared to calm Mrs. Dixon. She ushered them into the kitchen, where Paul recognized Bridget's son Mick, perched on a step-stool pushed up to the table. Another baby about his age sat in a high chair opposite, dressed in a spotless ruffled pink dress and playing in a bored sort of way with a bowl of applesauce. Not Mick, though. He was scooping up handfuls with loud cries of delight. His face and the dish towel around his neck bore evidence of a previous course that looked like carrots or maybe yams.

Mrs. Dixon bustled about, setting out cups and pouring from a coffee maker. The kitchen was as sleek and elaborate as any airplane cockpit, with spacious counters and every appliance known to man. Paul thought of the crumbling dinosaurs that marched through Bridget's kitchen.

"Did you want lunch?" Mrs. Dixon sat down with them. Her eyes strayed to the end of the counter where the applesauce jar was open beside a bowl of something cut up into cubes. A small container of yogurt stood there, spoon sticking up from its neck. "I can offer you some yogurt."

"No thanks," Paul said hastily before Bruno could get them into anything. He hated yogurt. In his mind it was a non-food, right up there with tofu, no matter how healthy it was supposed to be. It tasted nasty unless you filled it full of calories, and its slitheryness was enough to make anyone sick. "We just have a few questions we need to ask you."

Mrs. Dixon showed the whites of her eyes. "About what?" Her voice was a little higher. She used a corner of the dish towel to mop up Mick, trying to hide her face at the same time.

"There's no need to be nervous," Paul said, sipping his coffee. It was better than Claudia Kaplan's. That was all it had going for it. "We just need some background information on a few of the poets. Am I right in thinking that you're the mainspring of the group?"

He wasn't as good at pouring on the butter as Bruno was. But Melanie Dixon did thaw a bit. She didn't balk at a little gossip about Martin Hertschorn. She had some observations to make about Margery Lomax as well, having grown up in the same

Crescent Park neighborhood. But beneath the surface of her cocktail-party chat Paul sensed unabated nervousness.

Noticing one of Mrs. Kaplan's books on a bookshelf, he led the talk around to her. Melanie let malice show.

"Dear Claudia," she said, ladling more applesauce into Mick's dish. He plastered a big glob of it onto his face, mostly missing his mouth. "I know Bridget thinks the sun just rises and sets in Claudia. And of course," she said hastily, "Claudia has been wonderful to Biddy—encouraging her and everything. I think myself that publication in *PoetTree* made a big difference in the quality of Biddy's work." Mick banged his spoon against the bowl, and absently Melanie gave him more applesauce. "Of course, Biddy's never been on the receiving end of one of Claudia's grudges," she said, darting a sideways glance at Paul. "Poor Claudia can be very unforgiving if you get her back up, I'm afraid."

Bruno made a sympathetic sound. "Like Mrs. Lomax did, with her condos?"

"Oh I wouldn't dream of implying that Claudia—why, that would be absurd." Melanie shook out some laughter. No doubt about it, she was wound up tighter than an unused yo-yo. By the time they got around to Benji MacIntyre, she had peeled off half of the bright red apple on the applesauce jar in front of her.

"Oh, Benji." She laughed again. It didn't come off very well, and once more she fussed with the children, trying to conceal her unsteady hands. "Susana, honey, if you're finished it's time to get down." The little girl, pink dress still immaculate, toddled off toward an adjoining family room, where low shelves bore neatly-labeled bins of toys. Mick, freed from his dish towel, crawled after her. Moments later there was a loud crash.

"That Mick. I guess it's growing up in a house full of boys that makes him so—boisterous." Mrs. Dixon craned her neck to see through the family room door. "He'll have all the toys out on the floor in no time." Another crash nearly drowned out her words.

"Getting back to Benjamin MacIntyre," Paul said. "I notice that you rarely have any of his work in your magazine." He didn't wait for her nod. "Why is that?"

"Well, he's not a very good poet." Melanie Dixon went to stand by the family room door. "He's—poor Benji is sort of hopeless at everything he does. Not a good poet, not a good apartment manager." She frowned for a moment. "I hear he's an excellent cyclist, though. He tells me he's favored to win that big bike race that's coming up—the one where they ride over to the coast and back."

"Excuse me, where's the bathroom?" Paul followed her pointing finger, and left Bruno to finish the interrogation. Watching Mrs. Dixon's jerky gestures, the box of tissues she kept handy, he had been visited by a suspicion.

Moving down the hall, he ignored the obvious powder room, immaculate with color-coordinated guest towels and little soaps shaped like seashells. He found the master bedroom and allowed himself a moment to be overpowered by the huge bed, with its jungle-print down comforter and lacquered bamboo headboard, before penetrating into the bathroom via a dressing room with more closets than existed in his entire apartment.

The medicine cabinet in the master bath took a little time to find, concealed as it was behind an acre or so of mirrors. It had the usual jumble of patent nostrums and prescription bottles. But Paul was interested to count nine different kinds of nose drops. He began to open drawers in the vanity, poking through endless arrays of cosmetics. Finally, in a small drawer partially concealed by the vanity top, he found a significant collection of items. A dainty tortoiseshell-backed mirror. A dispenser of single-edged razor blades. Some brightly-striped sections of plastic drinking straws. And a small crystal container with a silver top. When he unscrewed the top, he wasn't surprised to see it nearly half full of a white powder.

She was fidgety when he got back to the kitchen. "Sorry to take so long," Paul lied shamelessly. "It's my bowels."

"Thanks for the information, Mrs. Dixon," Bruno said

hastily, responding to the flick of Paul's eyes toward the door. "We'll be back in touch if you can help us some more. And please, if you notice anything suspicious or out of the ordinary, just give us a call any time."

Paul glanced through the door at the family room, which looked as if a team of wreckers had been busy for a few weeks. Mick sat on the floor, surrounded by the devastation he'd wrought, a look of supreme satisfaction on his face. Susana gathered up armloads of toys, throwing them in the air. Her dress now looked as though she'd mistaken it for fingerpainting paper. A box of magic markers was over-turned on the floor, and the red one, lidless, bled into the pale grey carpeting.

They were just pulling away from the curb when Paul noticed Bridget's Suburban turn into Mrs. Dixon's drive. "Do you think she'll help pick up the toys?"

"Of course." Bruno shrugged. With children of his own, the devastation hadn't made much impression on him. "She's a nice person. Nice people always pick up their messes." He turned to Paul. "So what did you find while you were coping with your bowels?"

"Lots of nose drops and a hefty private stash," Paul said, heading for the office. "I doubt if we can trust a word she said."

"Oh, I don't know." Bruno patted his briefcase, where his notes of Mrs. Dixon's interview reposed. "She was telling the truth fairly often, I think. Wonder where she gets the coke."

"If the packaging had been there, I bet it would have looked just like what was in MacIntyre's duffle bag." Paul rolled his window up. Clouds were coming in, turning the warm spring sunshine back to cold murky winter. "My bet is on him for the dealer." He thought for a minute. "Or maybe even Martin Hertschorn. Neither of them seem to have an income-producing job. Hertschorn agitates for a living, and MacIntyre mooches."

"Maybe so." Bruno looked distressed. "I wouldn't like to

think that nice Mrs. Montrose is mixed up in drugs. She's too straightforward for that."

Paul shrugged cynically. "You're a romantic about women, Bruno my man. I see them clearly. No matter what they do, they have ways of justifying it so that it's okay that they did it. That's their idea of honesty."

They argued about it all the way back to the office. "I mean it," Paul said, turning into the parking garage under City Hall. Structural engineers had decreed that the building, one of the tallest in Palo Alto, needed upgrading to meet earthquake safety standards. "You realize," he told Bruno as he parked the car, "that in case of an earthquake our desks will probably end up right over there." He pointed to the locked area of the garage where all the recovered bicycles were kept.

Bruno refused to be distracted. "Sure, women sometimes tell social lies. Maybe fake an orgasm once in a while. But for what? Just to make the world run a little smoother, Paolo. Not because they care less about honesty than a man."

The elevator was working this time. "Enough," Paul said, punching the first floor button and hoping they would make it without getting stuck. "It was a good argument, but we need to get back to the case at hand."

There was no problem with that, though. The dispatcher flagged them down before they even made it across the hall.

"We've been trying to track you guys down," she said, waving a report form. "We got an urgent call from the hospital."

"Lucy," Bruno hollered, sprinting back toward the elevator.

"No, no, not your wife." The dispatcher looked down at the report in her hand. "You know that Martin Hertschorn you've been trying to get hold of? Well, the hospital emergency room just called. One of his neighbors brought him in. Some kind of drug OD." The dispatcher stared at them, her eyes round. "He's critical. You'd better get right over there."

# 17

BRIDGET WAS FEEDING spaghetti into boiling water when Sig showed up. "I'm not sure I want to let you in." She glared through the screen door. "You fink, you."

"Oh, don't be ridiculous." Sig pushed past her. "Have you heard about Martin?"

"What about him?" A picture of Martin's triumphant, unrepentant face rose in Bridget's mind. "Has he confessed?"

Sig shot her an unreadable look. "Only St. Peter knows now." She glanced around the living room, where Corky and Sam watched enthralled as Ernie bullied Bert on *Sesame Street*. Mick was preoccupied with pouring marbles from a plastic carton into a battered cowboy hat and out again. "Come into the kitchen and I'll tell you."

"Tell me what?" Bridget followed Sig into the kitchen, giving an absent-minded stir to the pot of spaghetti. She sniffed the sauce that occupied another burner, stirring it as well. "What's got into you, Sig?"

"Sit down." Sig plumped herself down at the table. "This is gonna shake you."

Bridget sat slowly, her eyes on Sig's strained face. "Something's the matter. Did—it wasn't Martin who—did it? He didn't—kill Mrs. Lomax?"

"Well, as a matter of fact, he might have," Sig said impatiently. "But that wasn't—"

"I can't believe it!" Bridget jumped out of her chair to turn down the heat under the spaghetti, which was boiling with too much enthusiasm. She couldn't sit back down, worrying about Martin. Instead she found herself clutching the chairback for support. "He meddled—he as much as admitted that he'd concealed evidence. But I can't believe he'd—"

"Just a minute." Sig lit a cigarette and regarded Bridget narrowly. "How do you know this?"

"Well, Martin told me this morning, of course. He made me promise not to tell, but I guess if they've arrested him it's a different matter."

"They haven't arrested him," Sig said baldly, taking a drag on her cigarette. "He's dead."

Black spots danced in front of Bridget's eyes. She felt heat rush through her body, leaving her icy in its wake. The wooden chair back cut into her hands. Dimly she could hear Sig's voice. The black spots faded. She took a deep breath, and knew she was going to throw up. She barely made it to the toilet in time.

"You didn't have to just come out with it like that!" Emery strode to the bathroom to dampen the washcloth again and brought it back, laying it solicitously on Bridget's forehead. "Are you all right, darling? You feel a little feverish." He sat on the bed beside her, his eyes full of worry. "I hope you're not coming down with the flu."

"I'm fine, I'm fine. It was just so unexpected . . . Poor Martin!" Bridget shook her head feebly and squeezed Emery's hand. "Thanks for looking after me, love. I don't know what made me loose my lunch like that."

"It was the shock," Sig proclaimed, hanging over the other side of the bed. "I'm sorry, Biddy, I really am. I tried to ease into it but you kept babbling about Martin confessing. I kind of thought you knew already."

"Was it suicide?" Bridget looked anxiously at Sig. From the living room came the strident sounds of the Sesame Street Band singing about being born to add. Mick crawled in through the partly open bedroom door and pulled at

Emery's leg, demanding to be picked up. Absently, Emery did so.

"Martin Hertschorn would never have murdered anyone, let alone himself," he said angrily. "Really, Sig. I don't know where you got this idea."

"From Paul Drake, that's who." Sig curled up and looked around for an ashtray. "He called to cancel our date for tonight. He was at the hospital then. After he hung up I called this guy I know in Admissions over there. He told me about Martin being brought in as an OD. He was in a coma, and they couldn't bring him around. He died a couple of hours after he got there."

Emery looked relieved. "So we don't really know anything. Chances are this whole thing is just made up of rumors and speculation—" He gave Bridget a little shake. "Don't look like that!"

"I saw him this morning," Bridget whispered. "I swear he had no thought of killing himself. He said—something about spontaneous confusion, and how Mrs. Lomax's murderer didn't deserve being caught." She pressed her fingers to her head, which throbbed horribly. "Should I tell Detective Drake? I'm just sure he had no idea of killing himself!"

"You tell him," Sig said briskly. "Personally, I think it's time we got to the bottom of it all. Otherwise—who'll be next?"

"Now that's enough," Emery said with authority. "Signe my dear, Bridget needs to rest now. If you don't mind—"

"Don't get all stuffy on me, Emery my man." Sig spoke brightly but Bridget noticed that her freckles stood out more clearly than usual on her white face. "I thought I'd go and feed your offspring, if you want to spend time with Biddy."

"Thanks, Sig." Bridget smiled wearily. "That would be nice of you. I'm sorry I—was snitty earlier. I should have known you wouldn't do anything mean."

"I wouldn't stoop to worming any secrets out of you, Biddy," Sig said darkly, "but if you have any, I strongly advise you to tell the cops. They're not such bad guys."

Emery snorted as Sig went out, closing the door behind her. "I always thought she had good sense, but honestly—" He rested his knuckles against Bridget's cheek. "You feel cooler now. Guess it was just the shock. Why, you haven't threatened to keel over like that since you got pregnant with Mick!"

"No," Bridget agreed dully, her mind on Martin's death. "I just can't take it in. Martin dead! Is it another murder? And if so, who is doing it?" She shivered. "I don't need to be lying down here anymore. I think I should call up Detective Drake and tell him what Martin said this morning."

Emery looked dubious, but he didn't try to stop her. Sig, dishing up spaghetti in the kitchen, supplied the number of Drake's office. He wasn't in, so Bridget left a message that she had something to tell him or Bruno Morales about Martin. But the sight of the kids doing unspeakable things to their spaghetti sent her rushing for the bathroom again.

Afterward she leaned, white and shaken, against the medicine chest, trying to summon the energy to rinse her mouth out.

Emery's earlier words came back to her. With a groan, she used the mouthwash and checked the calendar she kept in the bedroom.

When Emery came in to see what kept her, she raised tragic eyes to his.

"It's not just the murder," she gulped, "or murders, as the case may be. Emery, I think I'm pregnant. Again!"

# 18

IT RAINED ALL night, a damp and lugubrious outpouring that was a counterpoint to Bridget's feelings. She slept restlessly and woke often, resentful of Emery's not-quite-snoring oblivion. Her dreams were brief, horrifying mixtures of mayhem and motherhood that left her creeping at dawn into the bathroom to pee into a clean glass jar and brood over Martin's death. The bright red pimentos on the lid of the jar seemed insulting and callous. And she was callous too. She was shocked by Martin's death, horrified by its implications, grieved over its finality. But beneath all that she was preoccupied with her personal shock, the sense of betrayal she felt towards her body for getting her pregnant again.

The receptionist at the clinic was more pointed about it. Bridget had spent a lot of time in the waiting room through three pregnancies. Mick had been in just a month earlier for his one-year checkup. Now he perched on Bridget's hip and clamoured for the treat he imagined was in the paper lunch bag holding the pimento jar.

The receptionist accepted the bag incredulously. "What's the matter, couldn't you stop at half a volleyball team?"

"It's a surprise to us all."

"You don't look enthralled," the receptionist agreed bluntly. "If it's positive, when do you want to see the doctor? I could squeeze you in this afternoon."

"I'll let you know." Bridget didn't want to think about pregnancy management. Not now, anyway.

125

She stuffed Mick into his car seat, a process he had decided to resent for the day, and headed for Melanie's. She'd called the police department right after the kids had gone to school and scheduled an appointment with Paul Drake. If she got yelled at, as she thought she might, she didn't want Mick around.

Melanie opened the door promptly, but for once her perfect makeup looked wrong, maybe because under it her face was strained and pale. She laughed when she heard where Bridget was going, and her laugh was different too, stretched too thin. "Going to confess, Biddy? Police interviews every day—what have you been up to?"

Bridget looked at her curiously. "What have *you* been up to? You don't look too well. Should I take Mick with me?"

"Heavens no, I'm fine." Melanie fidgeted with the doorknob. "But I have to go out before lunch, and Lucia's off today, so don't be too long."

Still Bridget hesitated. "Don't tell me if you'd rather not, but—is something the matter?"

"Nothing's the matter really," Melanie said with another jangly laugh. "Just the usual—my life falling apart, et cetera."

"What's happened? Is Hugh—" Hugh Dixon was known to Melanie's friends pretty much by sight alone, although he always had a cordial word or two if met by chance. He was a class-A workaholic at the head of a busy venture capital firm. Hugh had no time for social life—barely time for family life. Melanie and a succession of au pairs raised the children while Hugh raised enormous quantities of money.

"Of course not." Melanie smiled with would-be gaiety. "I'd better get to the kids now."

It was crowded downtown and even the garage under City Hall was full. Bridget cruised for a while and then parked behind the library, telling herself she'd check something out after her police interview. It was comforting to think that the interview would be over soon. And she promised herself that before it was over she would know more about what was happening. Sig had been unable to tell her whether Martin's death finished the investigation of Mrs. Lomax's murder—or continued it.

Drake wasn't there, but Bruno Morales came out to show her down the hall to the criminal investigations department. He ushered her into his small cubicle and offered her a cup of coffee. When she declined, he got himself one, rubbing his eyes as he sat back down behind his desk.

"Sorry to yawn in front of you. We were at the hospital for hours, and then cleaning up the work here. My wife was furious with me." He grinned apologetically. "We're having another baby any time, and she wants me at home nights."

"I don't blame her." Bridget glanced at the children's drawings on the walls. "I think I know your wife. Lucy Morales, right? She's on the community child care board."

Bruno was delighted. "That's my Lucy, can't tie her down," he bragged. "Even a new baby won't put a crimp in her style." He recovered himself and pulled out a notebook. "I shouldn't be wasting your time like this. What did you want to see us about?"

Paul Drake came into the office, sipping distastefully at his own cup of coffee. "Morning, Mrs. Montrose. Bruno. What's happening?"

Bridget took a deep breath. "Sig told me about Martin."

Bruno reached over and patted her hand, his face distressed. "He was your friend. We're sorry."

Bridget gulped down the lump in her throat. The way she felt now, the lump would turn into nausea if she let it linger. "Well, I didn't tell you yesterday, but I saw Martin that morning."

Both men looked at her. Paul fished out his own battered notebook. Bruno turned on the tape recorder that sat on his desk.

"Mrs. Montrose, do you understand that this interview is being taped?"

Cowed, Bridget murmured her answer.

"Please speak as distinctly as you can. The microphone is

in the tape recorder. If it becomes necessary, we may stop and read you your rights."

"How come?"

Paul Drake's eyes were unreadable behind his glasses, but Bruno Morales gave her a worried smile. "In case you incriminate yourself, Mrs. Montrose."

Bridget sat up straighter. "Well, if stupidity is against the law," she began, but then she remembered Martin extracting that promise from her not to meddle. "If I'd come straight to you then, instead of leaving well enough alone—tell me, was Martin's death suicide?"

Again the two men exchanged glances, but something in Paul's body relaxed. "Why?"

"Because Melanie hinted—Sig thought—well, we all wondered if he'd killed himself from remorse because of pushing Mrs. Lomax out the window." Bridget forgot for a minute about the tape recorder. "Or at least Sig thought so. And I admit that if Martin were granted an opportunity to push Mrs. Lomax out the window, he might be—might have been capable of it. But I think if he had, he would have proclaimed it to the world." She looked earnestly at the men. "He was—eccentric. Ate snails, gardened mercilessly. He was a land-use fanatic. In court, he'd have looked even loonier than Dan White. I don't think Martin would have let other people be suspected for his own crime."

"So you don't think it was suicide then?" Bruno Morales leaned across his desk. "What's your theory?—All right, all right, Paolo." Drake had pointed to the tape recorder. "Never mind your theory for now. Just tell us about your conversation yesterday. Can you remember it?"

Bridget thought for a minute and then went through the conversation as faithfully as she could. At the end of her story there was silence in the little room. Both detectives were looking at her, Drake blankly, Morales with disappointment in his eyes.

"Is that all of it?" Bridget nodded and he switched off the tape recorder. "Oh, Mrs. Montrose. You knew this guy was supressing evidence. From the sound of it, his little bit of plastic told him who'd murdered Mrs. Lomax. It might have told us, too, if we'd gotten to it in time. And you let him get away with it."

"What could I do?" Bridget cried. "I advised him to go to the police." She looked at them, pleading. "If I'd told you, would Martin still be alive?"

"No, no." Paul Drake spoke briskly, even sounded a bit bored. "For all we know his death might be suicide. He might have a bit more to conceal from the police than he let you know. There's no way you could be responsible for his death in such a roundabout way."

There was something not quite reassuring about that. What Bruno said comforted her. "You gave him good advice, Mrs. Montrose. It wasn't up to you to see that he followed it. But I sure wish you'd told us, because it would have helped us a lot."

Bridget blew her nose and mumbled that she was sorry. She pretended not to notice Paul Drake's dubious sniff.

"And now," Bruno said, taking the cap off his pen. "You don't think he committed suicide. Why?"

"He—he just didn't talk like a person planning to end his life, or anything." Bridget shrugged helplessly. "I don't know. Would a man contemplating suicide be planting potatoes? They won't be ready to eat until May or June."

Paul Drake leaned forward. His bush of hair was wilder than usual, as if his hands had been burrowing in it for the past 20 hours or so. "Maybe something happened after he met you to make him want to commit suicide. Do you know anything about his personal life?"

"Not really." Bridget took a moment to think. "He went out with one or another of the poets—women, I mean," she added hastily. "Only women, as far as I know. He seemed to me to put his passion, for the most part, into his work. He worked tirelessly on land-use stuff." She smiled wanly. "Wherever there was a traffic barrier fight, or offices versus housing, or housing versus open space, there was Martin."

"How in the world did he live?" Paul shook his head. "This town is full of people who don't seem to need regular income. I wish I knew how they do it."

"He got grants once in a while," Bridget said. "I don't know. I never asked him what he did for a living. Some writing, I think—this and that. He was a man with lots of energy." She smiled suddenly. "I remember one night after an open reading, he walked Claudia and me all over town for half the night, propounding all these intricate schemes for mixing housing and retail space and playgrounds. Claudia and I finally stumbled home at two in the morning, but Martin was still going strong." The lump made another appearance in her throat. Bruno handed her a tissue and tactfully looked away.

They took her through a description of the little piece of plastic, and she did her best to sketch it for them. "I'm not much of an artist," she said regretfully, looking at her drawing. "And anyway, I hardly got a glimpse of it."

"It's something to go on, at least," Paul said, looking at the paper dubiously. "Thank you for coming in, Bridget. Your information is valuable, and you did the right thing."

Bridget, feeling that part of her overwhelming bundle of tension had dropped away, headed back across the street to her car.

And in the office she'd left behind, Paul and Bruno looked at each other. Finally Bruno said, "Don't you think you should have warned her, Paolo? After all, if Martin was murdered, it was probably because of this clue he concealed. Perhaps he confronted the killer, demanded money. Then, when the situation got dangerous, he might have tried to save himself by implying that Bridget knows the guilty secret." Bruno had worked himself up by this time. "What do you think will happen then?"

"Don't be ridiculous," Paul said. "Bridget's in no danger." Bruno looked at him. "I'll order increased patrol past her house," he said at last.

Bruno's face lightened. "Good idea, Paolo."

# 19

MELANIE WAS RARING to go by the time Bridget got back to pick up Mick. "Listen," Melanie said, hustling wraps onto Susana while Bridget did the same for Mick, "could you take care of Suse for a while? I have a doctor's appointment and I—can't put it off any longer."

"Sure," Bridget said, zipping Mick's jacket. "I'll take her home for lunch. There's an extra carseat."

"Thanks." Melanie seemed distraught.

"Is there—nothing seriously wrong, I hope?"

"That depends." Melanie laughed, a hysterical note creeping into her voice. "Listen, I'll tell you about it when I come to get Suse."

Bridget was so numbed by events that she couldn't even summon up a decent amount of curiosity. In fact, she didn't care if she never heard another stunning disclosure. Rather hoping that Melanie wouldn't choose to unburden herself, she climbed into the car and left.

The phone was ringing when she got her little charges out of their carseats and up to the door. She nearly broke her neck trying to maneuver through the toy-strewn living room to get the receiver.

"Congratulations," said the bright voice of the clinic receptionist. "You're getting another chance at a daughter."

That didn't tell her anything she didn't already know. But still, confirmation gave Bridget an curious mixture of feelings. She had always loved holding a tiny baby in her arms, but—there was already a baby occupying that spot in her life. She had a vision of night feeding, of piles of diapers stretching away into infinity. Lightheaded, she groped for a chair. "What if I decide on an—an abortion?"

"We refer those to a specialist," she was told. "Want me to schedule you?"

"No—well, not yet." Bridget stared at the kitchen floor, where Emery had been scraping old linoleum off the fir planking below, at the rate of one square foot a year for the past five years. "Thanks for calling. I'll let you know."

She made lunch for the kids, moving in a daze. Her mind kept running through the calamities of the past couple of weeks. It was overreacting to rank pregnancy up there with murder, but she didn't seem to be able to stop herself.

Mercifully, both children took a nap, Mick in his crib, Susana on the lower bunk surrounded by pillows. Bridget laid down on the couch, meaning to sort out her emotions. She still felt stunned when she thought of Martin's death—stunned and confused. If he committed suicide—why? If not, was it an accidental drug OD? She hadn't known him to be a drug taker, but she was not always as on top of the gossip as others in the writers' circle. That was a question for Melanie.

And if Martin was murdered—it was pretty obvious to Bridget why. He had concealed some evidence attached to Margery Lomax's murder. Perhaps he'd let the murderer know. It would have been just like Martin, to slip in a remark that indicated such knowledge. And if he had, and the murderer had felt insecure as a result—Bridget closed her eyes and abandoned speculation. It made her uneasy in ways she couldn't define.

Besides, she was sleepy. And if she'd learned one thing through the years of motherhood, it was to take her sleep when she could get it.

The kids were up, changed, and knee-deep in duplo blocks when Melanie arrived. She accepted a cup of tea and sat sipping it for a moment. The cup clattered in the saucer when she set it down.

"I'm going down to the Betty Ford Center tomorrow," she said. Bridget set her own teacup down.

"Melanie—"

"I'm addicted to cocaine." Melanie didn't look at Bridget. She looked straight in front of her at nothing at all and recited the words like she'd practiced them. "I started using it pretty heavily a few months after Susana was born. Even though I knew it was bad, I couldn't stop. So I'm going to go down and get rehabilitated." She laughed that dry scratchy laugh that was so unfamiliar.

"Melanie, stop!" Bridget leaned across the table and grabbed Melanie's hand. "How in the world did it happen?"

"I really needed it, Biddy." Melanie's eyes met hers and Bridget was shaken by the misery she saw there. "I wanted to feel in control again. I was so tired all the time, so inadequate. Susana was a difficult baby. She weaned herself at four months—she didn't like my milk—" She shrugged. "I know I gave you a lot of shit about weaning Mick, but really I envied you."

"Oh, Melanie—"

"So I started tooting a lot. Got my own supply. And it was wonderful, really. I felt alive again. I could do so much. Motherhood, meetings, book reviews—nothing was beyond me." Melanie smiled, but the brightness was gone. "Now I know I need to stop. But I want it all the time. Biddy, without coke—I don't know if I can manage."

Bridget jumped up and ran around the table to give Melanie a hug. "Of course you can," she said. "Nobody expects you to be Superwoman."

"I do." Melanie returned the hug but put Bridget's arms away gently. "And Hugh does, I think. He was proud of the way I handled everything before. Now, he's frightened." Her mouth twisted. "Frightened I might need him too much."

Bridget turned away to fumble with the teapot. "Hugh knows, then?"

"It's his idea for me to go down to the Betty Ford place." Melanie stared into the teacup. "After the detectives found my stash, I figured I'd have to tell Hugh. He was—shocked."

"I can imagine," Bridget murmured feelingly. "Wait a minute—what detectives?"

"The Hardy boys—you know." Melanie shoved the teacup away impatiently. "Drake and Morales. They came to talk to me the other day. Your pal Drake went and rummaged around in my bathroom." Her lips twisted. "Pretending it was a call of nature. I knew he was up to something. After they left I checked my stash, and it was arranged differently."

"But they didn't bust you or anything?"

"They had no warrant." Melanie gazed broodingly at Bridget. "I got rid of the cocaine in case they came back with one, and I decided not to get any more. But it's hard, Biddy. That's why I told Hugh. I wanted help."

"He's on your side," Bridget said. "He's recommended treatment."

"I know." Melanie's shoulders slumped. "Is it his fault if I need something from him I never asked for before?" She shook her head. "Now I'm not even making sense. I'd better get going."

"So what's going to happen—with the children and all?" Bridget started hunting for Susana's shoes and socks and jacket, which had been discarded at different points all over the house. "Can I do anything?"

"Hugh and Lucia can take care of all that," Melanie said uninterestedly. "Really, he needs to be more in touch with the children. I swear, if I were to die tomorrow Hugh wouldn't even be able to get the girls dressed to attend my funeral."

"Don't talk like that!" Bridget looked up from stuffing Susana's fat little feet into patent leather Mary Janes. "People don't die of drug rehab programs."

"They die of drug overdoses," Melanie pointed out, zipping Susana's jacket and heading for the door. "Or hadn't you noticed? You don't think Martin's death was an accident, do you?" She shivered. "I don't want that to happen to me, Biddy. I'm cleaning up my act."

"You—you believe Martin's death was murder? But Mrs. Lomax—"

"Take my word for it," Melanie said, her face pinched-looking, like she was on the verge of being ill. "I can't tell you how I know but I'm pretty sure Martin got mixed up in some drug deals." She looked over her shoulder on her way out. "You can tell your police friend if you want. Just don't tell him who told you. Maybe by the time I get back they'll have solved the case. I hope so."

"Wait a minute—Melanie!" But the door slammed shut. By the time Bridget could pick her way through the duplo blocks and over to the door, Melanie's BMW had roared off.

Bridget stared at the street for a full minute after Melanie had driven off. That load of nameless troubles that had rolled away after her police interview came back again, full of dark clamorous uneasiness that no amount of rationalization could disperse.

# 20

PAUL PUSHED HIS chair back from the desk and knuckled his eyes. "If I have to look at one more report—"

"Stop bitching," Bruno said absently, still reading the latest post mortem findings on Mrs. Lomax. "If everybody in the coroner's office hadn't gotten the flu, we would have gotten this days ago, instead of having to wait around forever. We might be closer to solving this case."

"You're right about that." Paul tasted the coffee left in his cup and made a face. "I'm bringing in my own coffee machine, I swear. This stuff is probably eating away my intestines."

"It's significant, about the legs," Bruno muttered, laying down the post mortem report. "That makes your theory a lot more likely, Paolo my man."

"Pretty clever of me." Paul turned his back and opened the desk drawer where he kept his food stash. He fumbled a teabag out of a colorful box and concealed it in his hand. But Bruno was on to him.

"What's that?" He made an elaborate show of sniffing the air. "Smells like—it is! Red Zinger! Paolo, when did you start drinking herb tea?"

"It was Signe's idea," Paul admitted, shamefaced. "She thinks I do too much caffeine."

Bruno nodded wisely. "So the little lady is starting to take care of you. That's a sign, Paolo." He picked up his own cup and got to his feet, stretching. "Is she accumulating a little padding for you?"

Paul headed for the bottled water dispenser, rinsing out his coffee cup and pressing the red button to get hot water on his teabag. "Give her a break, Bruno." He sniffed dubiously at the cup. "We've only been dating for a couple of weeks. She's not as skinny as she looks in her clothes," he added thoughtlessly.

"Fast work!" Bruno looked at Paul's clenched jaw and decided it was time to get back to business. "So the post mortem staining points to Mrs. Lomax being put in the dumpster after she'd been dead for several hours." He tapped a pencil on the desk. "Do you think Mrs. Montrose—"

"I suppose it's a possibility," Paul said, fishing the teabag out of his cup. "But a damned thin one, if you ask me."

Bruno picked up the list of Martin Hertschorn's personal effects. "When they searched Martin's apartment they found a pair of hiking boots." He gazed unseeingly at Paul's bulletin board, an untidy montage of dog-eared sheets out of his notebook, pinned up so they wouldn't get lost. "How did we figure it so far? Hertschorn was in the habit of prowling around half the night. He prowls over to sneer at the condos. Finds Mrs. Lomax, stiff on the ground there. Has the brilliant idea of heaving her into the dumpster to make a point." He scratched his head with the pencil. "That explains his statement to Mrs. Montrose that he'd confused the trail."

"Yeah, and that's when he found that doo-dad in her hand." Paul sighed. "If only he'd shown it to us instead of Bridget!" He wrung out the teabag and tossed it into the garbage. "So how did the murderer find out he had it?"

"Maybe we're making this too hard," Bruno suggested. "Could be the two deaths are unrelated. Maybe Hertschorn was a junkie and ODed himself."

"How long before we get the post mortem on him?"

"Who knows?" Bruno rummaged through the papers. "The secretary at the coroner's office told me they all have strep throat now. But the emergency room doctor did make a statement. Now where—oh, here it is." He perused his notebook for a minute. "He says that the drug used was cocaine, probably in solution, and he guessed a pretty stiff solution. Blood concentrations were high. Said aside from one needle mark, there were no tracks or other signs of injection." Bruno looked up. "I asked him about signs of abuse other than injection and he wouldn't tell me anything officially. But he admitted that Hertschorn's nose didn't look as though he'd been putting much coke up it."

Paul took the inventory of Hertschorn's apartment from Bruno's desk. "He had a sizeable stash, for all that."

"Could have been planted," Bruno pointed out. "Like the note."

"Ah, the note." Paul picked up the photocopy the lab had sent them. "No prints but Martin's." He read it to himself again, though he knew it by heart: *There is so much that is unnecessary.* "Not particularly a suicide message."

"But just the kind of thing that someone might use to make it look like suicide," Bruno said, frowning. "It's clumsy, Paolo."

"I agree." Paul took a cautious sip of his cooling tea and made a face. "This stuff tastes like something for livestock off their feed." He set the cup back down. "Didn't that ER technician say something about a lump on Hertschorn's head?"

Bruno flipped a couple of pages in his notebook. "I wish they'd have let us go over him," he grumbled. "Damn their stupid protocol. Here it is. 'Contusion behind left ear, no bleeding, some swelling.' "

"I'm with Bridget—Mrs. Montrose," Paul said slowly. "I don't believe that someone who's planting potatoes in the morning commits suicide in the afternoon. He was offed, and the murderer went as far as he could to make it look like suicide."

"Not far enough," Bruno said.

"There must be something, somewhere—" Paul scrutinized the inventory list again. "I've got something in the back of my mind," he groaned, "but I just can't bring it out. There's something . . . "

"Don't worry it," Bruno advised. "It'll come. Meanwhile, we need to get these reports cleaned up. Lucy will have my head if I'm not home for dinner." He looked worriedly at the clock. "She was cleaning the bathroom when I left this morning. When a woman who's so pregnant she can't bend over is scrubbing floors, it's a sure sign, Paolo."

"Uh huh," Paul said absently. "It's something to do with a list—I can almost visualize it." He began rooting through the papers on his desk. With a sigh of resignation, Bruno joined him. He knew his partner. Until that list was found, there'd be no reports finished, and no one would go home.

# 21

THE RAIN STOPPED just before dinner. Bridget stood at the kitchen sink, looking out on the glistening black paths of sidewalk and driveway, the redwood trees with their branches brought low by water. She felt angry somehow, and overstretched, and realized that with all the excitement she hadn't been able to jog for the past couple of mornings. Her newly-made muscles had protested this neglect by going cranky on her.

She put the taco fixings on the table, smearing a few beans on a tortilla for Mick. The older boys piled into their chairs with loud screams of gladness—tacos were favorites of theirs. Usually Bridget agreed, but tonight she had felt nauseated while frying the endless pile of tortillas, and the smell of the refried beans that she scooped out of cans reminded her too strongly of dogfood.

She toyed with a tortilla while Corky piled lettuce and tomatoes into his taco, and Sam began the usual dialogue with his. "Please don't eat me!" he squeaked, flapping the top half of the tortilla up and down like a mouth. "I love tacos," he growled, biting lustily into the still-squeaking tortilla. Emery repressed a smile, but it didn't amuse Bridget as it normally did.

"I need a walk," she announced, helping Mick to some shredded cheese and checking the milk pitcher. "You all go ahead and finish dinner. Corky, help Daddy with the dishes.

Sam, be sure to carry your plate to the sink when you're done."

"Do you feel okay, honey?" Emery's voice was concerned. He had tried to have a talk with her when he'd gotten home from work, but she had been up to her elbows in chopping tomatoes and lettuce and mediating a loud argument between Corky and Sam.

"I'm fine," she said automatically. She wasn't fine. She was functioning on remote control, unthinking, almost uncaring. The weight of the new life inside her was no more heavy than the grief and puzzlement she felt for the violent end of life that seemed all around her. "I—I have some thinking to do."

Emery walked with her to the door. "Look, honey," he said, zipping her sweatshirt up around her neck, "I don't mean to pressure you in any way. But—well, the thought of a new baby doesn't bother me in the least. In fact—I like it."

"Sure," she said bitterly, "you like it. You're not the one who gets to add another ten pounds to her collection of fat. Just tell me this—do you like it enough to get up in the night? Change messy poops? Stay chained to the house while another little baby crawls around teething on everything in sight?"

Emery drew back. "Hey, I've always done my share," he said, affronted. "I'm no stranger to getting up at night and all the rest of it." He leaned closer, and wiped away the tears that leaked from her eyes. "Oh, honey." She tried to hold herself stiffly, but it was hard to resist the comfort when his arms went around her. "I'm sorry," he whispered into her hair. "I know it's hardest on you. If you don't want to be tied down by another baby, I'll understand."

She sniffled and pulled away, wiping her nose on the sleeve of her sweatshirt. "You'd better understand to the tune of a vasectomy."

He winced. "We'll talk about it after you get back from your walk." She opened the door and cold, moist air rushed into the house. "Keep your hood up now," he instructed bossily. "And watch your step. It's slick out there."

The kerthunky sound of the milk pitcher going over came from the kitchen, followed by a volley of yells. "And in there too," she said with a malicious smile. Emery clutched his hair and rushed away, and she set off down the street.

The last of the grey light was fading. It cast a momentary lurid glow on the tops of the redwoods and bay trees that bordered San Francisquito Creek. She walked briskly for a few blocks, inhaling the wet, spicy smell of cedar and bay and eucalyptus, listening to the rush of water in the creek.

She stopped in the middle of the pedestrian bridge that spanned the creek, staring down at the fast, angry water boiling along a few feet beneath her. It had taken her some time after they'd moved to California to get used to the seasonal nature of creeks and rivers. Most of the year San Francisquito Creek's deeply-cut gorge was dry and dusty. But in the rainy season it made up for lost time, swirling swift and menacing toward its eventual destination in the Bay.

There was no sound but the rushing of the creek; even the wind had died with the light. She was alone in the greyness, alone with the life she carried. As yet its burden was imperceptible. But soon—soon it would be heavier, making itself felt with every movement, every gas pain, every kick in the ribs.

Above the murmur of the creek came noises from upstream—the crash and slither of someone forcing a way through the tangled jungle of underbrush that lined the creekbank. She kept still, having no desire to find herself in conversation with one of the street people who used the creek as a kind of open-air condominium complex. It wasn't unusual to stumble across a scruffy specimen curled up in the bushes, nursing a beer and a joint. Such an encounter last summer had led to her introduction to Captain Crunch and his not-so-merry band.

The noise upstream stopped, and she let her gaze drift across to the Menlo Park side of the creek, where some homeowner had been sandbagging like crazy to keep the water from taking his back yard. The creek had its own agenda, though. She could see the remains of a backyard fence dangling helplessly down the side of the gorge. The ground it had perched on had long since become silt at the bottom of San Francisco Bay.

Just like her plans for finding work that didn't involve children—under siege from natural forces. If she let herself be swept away, if she went with the flow, she could be buried by motherhood so deeply she might never dig her way out.

Sighing, she straightened. There was no use expecting enlightenment to hit like a bolt of electricity. She would go back home, tuck her children into bed, and talk it out with Emery. The cool damp air had at least blown away her bad mood; she felt she could discuss the whole thing without bursting into tears more than once or twice.

But as she turned to go her peripheral vision caught a glimpse of something falling into the water from upstream. She paused, craning back over the parapet to scan the muddy water beneath. If a kid was tossing stones into the creek, she hoped it was someone with sense enough to hold onto a tree trunk. There were stories every year about kids who fell into the creek, or even tried to swim or raft it in the rainy season. Many of those stories ended in tragedy. The water moved fast, faster than it looked. And there were treacherous snags of dead branches and debris that could trap a swimmer, hold a child helpless in the churning water.

Riding down the current was a small white blob, like a scrap of paper afloat on a sea of cocoa. Perhaps the unseen child was tossing paper boats into the water. She looked for another one, but the white scrap was alone. As it came nearer she could see that it wasn't a boat at all. It was small and trough-shaped, whirled by the current, nearly sub-merging ...

Incredulous, she ran back to the creek bank, her feet making hollow thunder on the bridge's wooden planking.

Maybe her eyes were playing tricks on her. How could that little piece of plastic, that important clue she'd glimpsed in Martin's pocket, be bobbing along the creek? She squeezed around the end of the bridge abutment and inched along the edge of the bank, holding onto an oak sapling. There it was, a white speck on the dirty water. It would go down any moment. If she had a long stick—no way, she told herself. The stick would have to be more than six feet long to reach down into the water.

In frustration she watched the little object, scooped and tossed by the current. It caught on a snarl of branches and debris, and she held her breath, hoping it was secure. She could run home and telephone the police, they could get some one down into the creek—but then the water pried it away from its stopping place and sent it on downstream.

Her shoulders slumped and she started to turn away, with one final look at the white speck. It was the last thing she saw before she felt a rush of movement nearby, and a bright star of pain exploded behind her ear.

# 22

PAUL WAS DOWN to bare wood on his desk without finding the list he sought. Bruno had made him file everything away as he came to it, and now his office was depressingly neat. Bruno was finishing up the paperwork, incorporating reports that had littered Paul's desk.

"So that puts Fred Lomax out of it," Bruno said, making a notation. "Miss Dart's nosy neighbor not only saw him leaving at 7:30 that morning, she saw Allison creeping out the night before. Says she was back before Johnny Carson came on. That doesn't give Allison time to follow Mrs. Lomax to the construction site and dump her out the window. And Allison alibis Fred for the rest of the night. Guess they're both out of it." He shook his head. "What a neighbor to have. She watches poor Miss Dart's every move—calls her the Adulteress. You can hear the capital A." He grinned at Paul. "Miss Dart is not my idea of a scarlet woman."

Paul nodded absently. His hands were behind his head, feet up on the bare expanse of desk. The information he needed was on the tip of his mind.

"Melanie Dixon's gone out of town." Bruno frowned over that piece of paper. "Didn't anyone tell her to stay put till we were through?"

"Guess she figured she wasn't really in the investigation." Paul recrossed his ankles, left over right. "Signe says Mrs. Dixon thinks she's a law unto herself."

"Claudia Kaplan really is one," Bruno told him, putting the

145

report on Melanie at the bottom of his pile. "Did you get time to read that stuff she was writing about Mrs. Lomax? Whew!" He pantomimed touching a hot stove. "Wouldn't want to have her mad at me."

"Did she have opportunity?"

"No alibi." Bruno shrugged. "Just the 'I was at home alone' stuff that most people have." He looked at Paul with the mournful gaze of a hound. "I don't like the way it's linking up, Paolo."

Paul knew what he meant. "Just because Bridget happens to be involved in both deaths—I mean, she's not the only common factor, you know."

"Not as a suspect, no." Bruno fidgeted with his own stack of reports. "But—it has to do with her, somehow. She finds the first body. Her friends are among those implicated. One of them dies, injected with a lethal cocaine solution, a few hours after telling her he's supressing evidence in the first case." He stopped long enough to take a swig of the herb tea Paul had despised. "Ah, what's the use. We've been over it so many times. Somehow Mrs. Montrose is in the middle of this. I think we should talk to her again."

Paul pushed the reports away and stretched. "What time is it, anyway? I'm getting hungry."

"You're always hungry." Bruno consulted his watch. "Six-thirty. Maybe we could get a sandwich, then give her a call. Ask her to come over to the office, or we could go to her place."

"Good idea." Paul got to his feet and reached for his jacket. The phone rang next door in Bruno's office. Bruno went to answer it and was back almost immediately, gibbering with excitement.

"It's Lucy. The baby's coming. I mean, it's coming right away! Drive me home, Paolo—I left the car for her this morning. She doesn't think there's time to get to the hospital!"

They raced for the stairs, not trusting the elevator. Paul gunned the car around the corners. Bruno's house, a cottage on Webster, had lights in every window. Several women popped out of different rooms when they opened the door, all of them pointing toward the back of the house. Bruno rushed away and Paul hung around in the hall, wondering if he could be of use.

"Pretty exciting." One of the women bustled past him towards the kitchen. "I'm getting some food together. She'll be hungry after the baby comes."

"She's going to have it here?" Paul looked around nervously. If food was going to be available he wanted to stick around for it. But the thought of a baby being born in such close proximity was daunting.

"She'll never make it to the hospital. I'm her neighbor, by the way. Sandra Filbert." She gave Paul's nerveless fingers a quick shake. "We got hold of the childbirth teacher, and the doctor said she'd try to make it." Sandra shrugged. "Want to give me a hand with the food?"

"Sure," Paul said dazedly. Maybe he could revive himself with a sandwich.

There was a sound from the back of the house, a triumphant shout from Bruno.

"Thar she blows," said Sandra, grinning like a maniac. "You open the champagne."

Paul had never realized that the scene of a childbirth could support a party like the one going on all over Bruno's house—a quiet celebration for the new parents in the back room, and a more boisterous event in the front of the house with what looked like a cast of hundreds. He had gotten his peek at the new little Morales, sustaining quite a shock at her splotchy, jowly appearance. It helped that everyone who came in—and there were many—brought something to eat. He munched a really excellent brownie bursting with walnuts and decided it was time to head back to the office. Bruno would be taking some time off, as who could blame him, which landed a lot of extra work squarely on Paul's shoulders. The sooner he got started with it, the sooner he'd be done.

He pushed his way past the crowd around the food and into Bruno's bedroom. Lucy sat up in the bed, wearing a ruffly thing. Bruno held the new baby. Both of them were beaming.

"Uh, Bruno? I'm going now. Congratulations."

"Paolo, I know there's a lot to do. I won't take all my leave. I'll be in later on."

"Don't bother doing that," Paul said with affection. "You stay here. Take the evening off. Hell, take the whole night off. You don't have to come in until tomorrow morning."

"Such generosity." Lucy Morales wrinkled her nose at him. She was small, and nicely put together when she wasn't pregnant. He felt wistful.

"What are you naming her?" The baby didn't look quite so splotchy now, or maybe he was getting used to it.

"I vote for Flora," Bruno put in. Lucy laughed at him.

"Flora Morales. Cute, Bruno." She turned to Paul. "Emma Francesca, for her grandmothers."

"Well, rest up now. See you later, Bruno."

"Hey, don't forget to call Mrs. Montrose, Paolo."

"Oh, yeah." That was all he needed. Another look at a happy family to make him yearn for what he hadn't got.

He headed for his car, trying to supress thoughts of Signe. She was funny and honest, and she made no bones about what she wanted from him. She didn't expect to get married, or even to keep seeing each other. She just wanted a baby— and she was willing to share the baby, too.

He could have fatherhood without the responsibility of maintaining a relationship. That was the hard part, as he knew from his experience of marriage. What Signe offered should be ideal.

But put against what Bruno had, or what Bridget had, it looked shallow and isolated. Why should two people united in the care of children look for ways to keep themselves apart?

Shrugging, he parked his car in the city hall garage and took the elevator, not being pressed for time. At least the whole question with Signe could wait until this investigation was tied up. The way things were going now, that would only be a year or two.

He dialed Bridget's number first thing, to keep from forgetting it. Her husband answered the phone.

"Why no, she isn't here, Dectective Drake. She went out for a walk about an hour ago and hasn't come back." Emery Montrose's voice sounded hesitant. "Actually, I'm getting a bit worried. It's almost bedtime for the kids, you see. She never misses that."

"She went for a walk?" Drake felt a ripple of fear, as if someone had chucked a rock into an icy lake in his midsection. "Damn—hold on." He put Emery Montrose on hold and dialed the dispatcher for reports from the extra cruisers that were patrolling Bridget's neighborhood. None of them had seen anything unusual. He remembered the nebulous list he'd been looking for, and a glimmer of the truth dawned on him. "Damn and blast, the shoes!" He punched the blinking light of Emery's line. "Mr. Montrose? I'll be right there."

# 23

SHE WAS FALLING, floating in the moist cool air. It parted for her, enclosed her.

She hit water and her eyes opened wide with the shock of it. Reflexively she breathed, and then she was under.

The world was full of icy water, and the water was full of hard, hurting things. Bridget felt air on her face and managed one more gasping breath before she was sucked down again, whirled and tossed like a weightless toy by the force of the creek. Water filled her nose and the silent scream of her mouth.

Choking, she was lifted up once more and opened her eyes on watery chaos. A hefty tree branch crashed in front of her, entangling her. This time her scream was audible. Another branch hurtled down behind her, enclosing her in a prison that slashed and scraped and gouged, until she curled into a ball, trying to protect herself, trying to save the seed she carried within her.

She summoned wit enough to remember what she'd learned about fast water the time she and Emery had gone white-water rafting together. Put your feet downstream. Go with the water. Look for something on shore to hold onto.

It was good advice, she supposed, but impossible to use. The rubble that battered her, the branches that chivvied her, would not let her think.

Something huge and hard crashed down, glancing off her shoulder. If not for her twiggy prison, which had taken most

150

of the blow, it might have crushed her. As it was, it broke her partially free of confinement. She struggled feebly to push away the rest of the brush that surrounded her. One of the limbs whacked a a tender place on her skull that exploded stars of pain inside her.

Of course, she'd been hit. She'd been pushed. Those were facts that her mind struggled with on one level, while her body fought for survival.

Another missile whistled past, barely missing her head. This time she could take it in, she could see that it was a piece of broken cement, once part of a sidewalk. Looking up toward the creekbank was like looking at another world. Up there, someone was throwing something on the order of Jove's thunderbolts. Someone was trying to kill her.

The realization was so overwhelming that she lost her grip on the battle for survival. Tree branches seized her once more and dragged her down, catching her, holding her where her enemy could hurl missiles until they found their target.

Her tears of pain and fear were lost in the swirling water. The turbulence around her made an answering chaos in her head. Her feet touched bottom, scrabbled for it again, lost it. Her arms battered the malevolent branches that held her down. Somewhere in her was the feeling that if only she could summon the energy, the wits, she could save herself. But slowly arms and legs and lungs succumbed to torpor, unmoveable except by express command. And that she was unable to give.

Another piece of concrete crashed into the logjam that restrained her, breaking it apart. The water tore her away, swirling around a bend, bouncing her off a boulder with grim playfulness. Air found its way into her grateful lungs. Terror made her limp, complaisant. The bars of a rusty shopping cart seized her ankle and held her while the water found tree limbs to use as battering rams against her.

The current took her again, wrenched her ankle free. The pain was immense, but it was just one more pain. The water was quieter here, but no less swift. She found herself by instinct in a fetal position. Ahead the creek widened, the water appeared calmer. But there was nothing to hold onto, no shallow spots to beach herself. She would stop fighting the water. She shouldn't be fighting it. Water was an element—it would be her element. If she gave in, everything would slow down, the wild whirling would cease. She had only to let go, to relax . . .

When the water pushed her onto the sandbank she was too numb at first to understand her tenuous safety. She opened her eyes, cringing in expectation of another bolt from the heavens. There, ahead of her in the little bay, bobbing against the sandbank that cradled her, was the small white object she sought. Her fingers closed over it tightly, and she let herself sink back down into the cold, shivery darkness that claimed her.

It might have been hours later, or minutes, when she was seized and roughly shaken. She cried out, whether for the loss of her new element or the pain that hammered through her she couldn't tell.

Voices argued in a muffled din over her head, and she realized her ears were clogged. Hands grabbed her, carried her. She put an arm across her belly, took a deep breath, and tried to faint.

"Hey, lady." Someone shook her again, sending exquisite jabs of agony through her battered body. She uttered a noise of protest and dragged her eyes open.

There was light, coming from somewhere. Above her hung a pale, hostile face, surmounted by a wild shock of something she took for feathers, before she realized that it was tufts of hair dyed different colors—purple, orange, black, and an anemic-looking platinum. She closed her eyes again.

"Mrs. Montrose! Wake up! Or I'll throw you back in!" With every jolt of her shoulder, pain ripped through her. She moved her head and tried to focus. This time she recognized the face beneath the hair.

"Captain Crunch." She made the words with her mouth, but couldn't manage to get them into the air. She tried once more, with better success. "New hairdo."

The captain scowled at her. "So, Mrs. Montrose. What the hell are you doin' in the creek this time of year? Don't you know it's dangerous?" His eyes wandered with detachment down her body. "Ain't never seen you wet before."

"She's gonna croak on you," another voice said petulantly. "Toss her back now before the cops pin it on us."

"She ain't gonna buy it." Captain Crunch turned his glare toward the unknown voice. "Where's the Mad Dog?"

There was muttering behind him. Shivering uncontrollably, Bridget looked beyond his brilliant top-knot and tried to take in the surroundings. The light came from a lantern on top of an old orange crate. There was a moldy-looking couch with bursting cushions and an uneven floor covered with incredibly dirty carpets, on one of which she was laid out—prematurely, she hoped. The walls were dirty too, and glistening with damp. She was in a cave.

The other man shuffled forward with a bottle in one hand. She recognized him as one of the street people who hung around a downtown park in the daytime, cruising restaurant dumpsters for food. His hair was shaved, except for some long matted hanks sprouting erratically from his skull. He wore ragged layers of coats and ancient boots that didn't match. Handing over the bottle, he sprawled back on the ratty couch.

Captain Crunch yanked Bridget upright enough to pour the contents of the bottle down her throat. Luckily it was almost empty. She gasped and gagged as it burned into her stomach.

"What was that?" she choked out.

"Mad Dog Twenty-twenty." The Captain grinned, revealing that he didn't spend much time in the dentist's chair. "Don't ask what's in it. You didn't get enough to kill you." He propped her up against a pile of sandbags. "What were you doing in the creek? It ain't swimming season."

She could see the opening of the cave now, a low arch with the rush of water beyond it. "I didn't know there were caves in the creekbank."

"Lots of 'em," the Captain remarked succinctly. "But this is one of the few that don't get flooded out in rainy season. That's why the Grim Reaper was here to haul you out."

"You got her out, man." The Grim Reaper shook his head. "I ain't takin' the credit for it." He fixed Bridget with a brooding glare. "Too many uppity women in the world right now, without we go around savin' em, for God's sake."

"How in the world did you do it?" Bridget turned wondering eyes on the Captain, who actually appeared to blush.

"It wasn't anything, so don't go slobbering all over me," he said graciously.

"See," said the Grim Reaper, who had taken a pull out of his own bottle, "there's a handy little set-up down there." He crawled out of his couch and over to the door of the cave. "Everythin' that comes down the creek hangs up on my sandbar." His voice, though slurred, was proprietary. "In the rainy season I like to sit here and watch the stuff come down. If I see something I like I just slide down and get it." He took another swig from his bottle. "Got my sofa that way," the Grim Reaper bragged, "hardly wet at all. It was just floating along. Kind of like you were doing."

"So you saw me and pulled me out?" Bridget inched to the door of the cave where she could see the water pouring around the sandbank. "Stuff doesn't seem to stop there for long." She shivered, watching an old flower pot hesitate at the sand bar and get swept away. Her hand clenched on the piece of plastic she still held, and she glanced at it uninterestedly. "I'm lucky you got down in time."

"Oh, we were already down there." The Grim Reaper became positively loquacious under the influence of his bottle. "This time of year I harvest my firewood. Pile it up, and by May it's ready to burn."

Captain Crunch made derisive sounds. "You saw a whiskey bottle floatin' along, and thought it might be full. That's why we went down there."

The Grim Reaper took exception to this. "You callin' me a liar, Cap'n?" He advanced on the Captain with menace in his face.

Bridget's teeth chattered with reaction and cold. "Thank you anyway," she said faintly, wanting to avert a fight. "You saved my life. Thank you."

"Hey, no sweat, lady." The Reaper resumed his couch and raised his bottle in salute, looking at it regretfully. "You were more interesting to collect than firewood. But now that you're collected—well, do we use you, or what?" He had another swig and looked at Bridget with an expression that made her shrink. "I ain't had a woman in ages except for Neutron Woman. Bet *you* ain't got no social diseases."

Bridget sat up quickly and shrieked at the pain that action caused. "Either I'm having a miscarriage," she moaned, "or all my ribs are broken."

"You don't want to fuck her," Captain Crunch told the Grim Reaper. "She'd tell the cops unless you killed her afterwards, and there's no fucking that's worth killing over."

"True enough," said the Reaper with philosophic resignation. "Well, in that case, get her out of here, willya? The sound of her teeth chatterin' is disturbin' my peace."

Bridget had another tot out of the bottle and clawed her way up the muddy path that led up the creekbank. It seemed incongruous to step away from the creek and see the neat little bungalows, their windows throwing lighted parallelograms onto manicured lawns.

Captain Crunch let her rest against a tree for a minute. She was in a state somewhere between petrification and numbness, unable to take in the events of the night. It seemed miraculous just to be able to put one foot in front of the other. Every breath was a dull ache through her body.

"So what were you doing in the creek?" Captain Crunch pulled out a crumpled cigarette and lit it. The sweet smell of sinsemilla drifted toward Bridget. He took a pull and held it out to her, and her hand was putting it to her lips before she realized it was happening. As an analgesic, combined with alcohol, it was superb. She drew the smoke deep into her lungs. The aching was still there, but she didn't care any more.

"I was pushed," she said dreamily, and then her words shocked her sober. She handed the joint back to the Captain and patted the pocket of her jeans, making sure the little piece of plastic was still where she'd put it. "Someone hit me on the head and pushed me." She glanced around fearfully, expecting to see assassins lurking behind every tree. "I need to go to the police."

"You'll go alone," the Captain said, holding in the smoke while he talked. "I'll walk you home, or to a phone. Then you're on your own."

She waved the joint away when he would have passed it back to her. "I—I'm grateful," she began.

The captain wanted none of her gratitude. "Save it," he said. "I figure I owed you one. We got hassled a lot by the fuzz before that article you wrote came out." He took another hit and talked through it. "Of course, some rednecks came down and trashed our spot by the railroad bridge after you fingered it for all the world to read about," he added. "So don't get a swelled head." He stubbed out the joint and put it carefully away in a matchbox. "Now you can owe me one."

The air was cold and Bridget was wet through. Shivering, she tried to talk through her chattering teeth. "I'll pay you back." He started walking and she stumbled after him, hugging her arms for warmth. "A coat!" she said, inspired. "Emery has this parka he never wears. Would you find it useful?"

There was a gleam of interest in the Captain's eyes. "Sounds like one I ripped off a few years ago," he said offhandedly. "Sure, I'll take it."

It didn't surprise her that he knew where she lived. After all that had happened, it seemed to Bridget the height of unreality that she should emerge from her watery grave a few short blocks from her house. Her adventure in the creek began to assume a dreamlike air of unreality. Except for her sodden clothes, and the bruises that would no doubt cover her, it might have happened to another person. She could have collapsed with relief, if she hadn't known that a murderer might still be looking for her.

As it was, she needed to get in touch with the police as soon as possible. The few blocks to her telephone couldn't be too short for her. She thought about knocking at one of the cozy bungalows and asking them to call the police. But a glance at her sopping sweatshirt and grimy hands changed her mind. She would go home and call them and then climb directly into a hot shower. Emery would be wondering where she was.

# 24

CAPTAIN CRUNCH was delighted with the parka, even though it had a huge coffee stain on the front where Emery had been surprised by a raccoon one night at Big Sur. "If it looked too good," he explained to Bridget, checking out the velcro flaps of the pockets, "the cops would hassle me for stealing it."

"Not this time," Bridget said. "Just tell them to call me if there's trouble." She pumped his hand, her eyes filling with tears. "I can't thank you enough."

"Ah, stow it," he mumbled, looking away. "Glad I was there. Next time you fall in the creek, you mightn't be so lucky."

"I won't fall in again," Bridget promised fervently.

She locked the door after the captain had left, wondering where everyone was. The kids should be in bed by now, and Emery should have been pacing the floor. Instead, the house was empty.

The shower beckoned seductively, but she dialed the police before she let herself think about its warm promises. She was absurdly disappointed to find that Paul Drake was gone.

"He tore out of here a while ago," the dispatcher told her. "Can I give him a message?"

"It's very important," Bridget said, trying to squeeze some of the water out of her hair with a kitchen towel. "About the Lomax case."

"Okay, shoot."

Bridget found that she didn't know where to begin. "My name is Bridget Montrose," she said finally, "and somebody just hit me on the head and pushed me into the creek. Somebody just tried to kill me."

The dispatcher didn't sound impressed. "Uh huh. Where are you calling from?"

"From my house," Bridget said impatiently. "What did you think, there are phone booths in the creek? Can you get hold of Drake?"

"I'll have to see about that," the dispatcher said primly.

"Or Bruno Morales—he's working on it too."

"His wife just had a baby. A little girl!"

"How nice," Bridget said helplessly. She gave up on the kitchen towel and tossed it toward the back porch where the washing machine stood.

There was a snapping sound from the phone receiver, and then nothing. Bridget stared at it in disbelief. "How dare you hang up on me," she muttered, jiggling the hook up and down. There was no response. The doorbell sounded.

She hung up the phone and went to the door. Maybe it was Emery, having forgotten his key. The numbness that had filled her after her escapade was fading, replaced by a frightened uneasiness that made it hard for her to think. Where was her family? Who was trying to kill her?

Benji stood on the porch. She shook back her dirty hair and unlocked the door. "Come on in," she told him. "Have you seen Emery around?"

Benji shook his head, following her into the living room. "I haven't seen anybody."

She picked up the phone again. "I have to make a call," she told Benji. The phone was still silent, without even a dial tone.

"Were you talking to the police?"

"I was trying to." Disgruntled, Bridget hung up the phone again. "I can't talk now, Benji, I have to take a shower."

"Looks like you already did."

"Not exactly." She headed for the teakettle, knowing from experience that once Benji settled in for a stay he was hard to dislodge.

Then some instinct raised the hairs on the back of her neck. She turned to look at Benji, lounging in the kitchen doorway. "How did you guess," she whispered, licking suddenly dry lips, "that I was talking to the police?"

His expression didn't change. "What else would you do after being pushed into the creek?"

This time it took her two tries to bring out the words. "How—how did you know—"

"That you'd been pushed?" He smiled, his eyes still empty of emotion. "How do you think?"

She backed toward the stove, her mind a total blank. She couldn't think, didn't want to think. She wanted to wake up. It was only a dream, the kind that sent a surge of fear through you right before you woke up.

There was the telephone. Her hand moved slowly, as it does in dreams, to pick up the receiver and bring it to her ear. Still no sound. "You—you cut the phone line," she said blankly.

"The phone box is right next to your front porch." He took a step towards her, his face growing intent. "It was just a precaution. I didn't realize you would be talking to the police. They might be smart enough to put two and two together, so I want to finish up here quickly."

"Finish up . . . quickly." Bridget parroted his words, feeling the fear break and eddy within her. He was going to kill her.

If he had a gun, he would shoot her dead. If he had a gun . . . She glanced around frantically. Even if she had a gun it would be useless to her, since she didn't know how to use it. If he had a gun, she was dead. But if he didn't—

She grabbed a knife from the knife block. Fear was her friend now, galvanizing her to action. "Don't come near me," she warned him. He took one more step, watching her stolidly from those big brown eyes.

"Bridget," he said, shaking his head at her intransigence. "You should have let yourself drown. I hear it's a peaceful death."

"A lot more peaceful than yours is going to be if you come near me," Bridget snarled. She brandished the knife threateningly.

"You won't use that," Benji said, as if reasoning with a child. "I know about your views. No guns allowed, even toys for the kids to play with. No violence because of bad karma." He smiled sweetly and came closer. "I quite agree with you about the guns." He moved another step. "I didn't need them, did I? I got rid of Aunt Margery without a gun. I got rid of Martin too, the stoolie. And you—" he shook his head again. "I planned such a pleasant death for you. Too bad you screwed it up."

*Keep them talking.* In murder mysteries, the incipient victim was supposed to keep the murderer talking. "Why, Benji?" She tried to sound calm, interested. "Why did you kill your aunt?"

"I didn't mean to," he said, a frown clouding his face. "But she was going to tell. She walked in on me the other day when I was doing a line, and she was going to tell."

"Tell who? What?"

He shook his head at her stupidity. "The race organizers. She was going to tell them that I took cocaine. Then they'd give me a blood test, and I'd be disqualified." The frown deepened. "I'm going to win that race, Biddy. Nothing will stop me. It made me mad when she said that, and I grabbed a piece of wood and hit her, and then I knew she'd really be angry so I pushed her out the window."

"At the Dark Tower—the condominiums?" Bridget wondered how hard it would be to stick a knife into human flesh. Before her imagination could make her sick, she switched off that train of thought. "What were you doing there?"

"Aunt Margery dragged me over there to get me to work for her," Benji said uninterestedly. "I told her cycling took too much of my time for me to work all day, and then she said that about getting me disqualified from the race. Now if I win the race I can get them to see that cycling is my career, and then I'll get the money she left me." His eyes clouded over for a moment. "It's not much money. I would have thought she'd be more generous." He smiled again. It didn't warm his eyes. "Ironic, isn't it. She'd be infuriated if she knew I could get that trust fund by bike racing."

"Cocaine," Bridget said, hoping desperately that the police dispatcher had smelt a rat and sent a patrol car racing for her house. "Say, you must be Melanie's source."

"You know about that?" He brooded for a moment. "I guess Melanie will have to go too."

"Benji," Bridget said, horrified. "You can't do that. You can't go around killing everyone who threatens you." She let a hysterical giggle escape her. "I don't even know why you want to kill me!"

"You saw me throw the chin guard into the creek," he said simply. "You would have told the police."

"I didn't," Bridget began automatically, then stopped. "It was a chin guard, that little piece of plastic. Like on a bike helmet—your bike helmet."

"Didn't you know?" He brushed it away. He still wore his cycling helmet, the straps dangling where he'd unfastened it. She willed her hand not to touch the pocket of her jeans. If he killed her, if he didn't find the chin guard, the police would know. Martin had known, when he'd seen the little piece of plastic, that it was off a bicycle helmet. Only Benji would have been wearing one in the Dark Tower.

"Oh well," Benji said, "I would have killed you anyway. I can't risk anyone telling the police about what Martin found. That's why I killed him."

"Over a chin guard?" Bridget tried to make her voice soothing. "It could be anyone's. There's nothing to tie it to you, is there?"

"Only Martin's story of finding it in Aunt Margery's hand. He told you that, didn't he? He said he did. I knew then I'd have to kill you both." Benji glanced absently around the kitchen, as if checking for adversaries. "I got a little confused right after I hit her. She grabbed for my helmet just before she fell but I didn't realize she'd gotten the chin guard until I got home. Then when the police didn't find it, I figured nobody had noticed it.

"I was puzzled," Benji admitted in a reasonable voice, "by the dumpster. I knew she hadn't fallen into it. Then Martin congratulated me on pushing her out the window. He showed me the chin guard, told me he'd found it in her hand." He turned those opaque eyes on her again. "He said I was a public benefactor, but I knew I couldn't trust him. He might have gone to the police, showed it to them. I had to kill him. I have to kill you. You're really putting me to a lot of trouble," he complained, moving toward her.

"My apologies," Bridget said, snapping back into awareness of the danger she was in. "Get any closer and you'll find out why they call this a boning knife."

"Weapons are so easy to take away," Benji told her, scaring her even more with his very reasonableness. "And then they can be used against you. That's why I never use weapons." He advanced another step, patting his breast pocket. Bridget saw the end of a hypodermic sticking up. "It won't hurt," he assured her. "Just a little prick, and it's over."

Bridget lost her head and threw the knife at him. He ducked easily. But she grabbed a cast iron skillet off the pot rack and he stopped his rush toward her, eyeing the skillet.

"I'm stronger than you are," he said conversationally. "I'll overpower you in the end. You're too weak to hold out after almost drowning."

She knew he was right. She was backed up against the cabinet with nowhere to go. Already her arm trembled with the effort of brandishing the skillet. She groped behind her with her free hand, hoping to find something, anything, that would balance the odds in her favor. "It won't do you any good, you know," she gasped. Her hand passed along a row of cleaning products. She made herself speak normally. "I've talked to the police. I told them your name."

A spasm of annoyance crossed Benji's face. "I don't believe you. But I'll just have to take that chance. I don't want to be arrested until after the race. It won't matter to you," he pointed out. "You'll be dead."

He raised his hand with the hypo in it. She sent a last desperate look toward the front door. "That won't work," he said, amused. "That's the oldest trick in the world."

'Right," she said breathlessly. "There's nothing there. Nothing at all!"

He paused, suspicious, and couldn't resist turning to glance through the living room. Bridget seized a spray bottle of bathroom cleanser. She thrust it out and squirted it straight into Benji's face as he turned back to her.

"Ow! You—" He staggered, trying to claw the caustic cleanser out of his eyes. Her arm felt pretty feeble when she brought the cast iron skillet down on his head. But it made a very satisfactory clunk anyway.

She was still staring down at Benji's sprawled form on the kitchen linoleum when Emery burst through the doorway, his hair standing on end like a forest fire, his face creased with anxiety.

"Biddy! Thank God—"

Paul Drake followed him through the door. Bridget looked at them both, wondering why they seemed so far away. "Is he dead?" she asked in a thin voice. Everything was indistinct, as if it were raining grey popcorn. The skillet fell from her hand and bounced off Benji's recumbent ankle.

Just before she fell, Emery caught her.

# 25

IT WAS A long bath, with lots of baking soda in the water, ending with a shower to get the creek out of her hair. Afterward Bridget submitted to the scrutiny of her doctor.

"Only minor damage," the doctor said after the exam, perching for a minute on the side of Bridget's bed. "Everything's fine, and no signs of losing the baby." She cocked an eyebrow at Bridget. "Is that good or bad?"

"Good, I think." Bridget smiled and snuggled into her pillows. "Nice of you to make a house call."

The doctor shrugged. "I was out anyway, for Lucy Morales. She broke up my dinner date and then didn't even have the courtesy to wait until I got there before she had the baby."

Bridget snorted. "You would have made her go to the hospital. I bet she called you late on purpose."

The doctor rolled her eyes piously. "No power on earth could have gotten that woman to the hospital. Now, when your time comes—"

"I'll let you know," Bridget said, closing her eyes. "Lucy's way sounds pretty good to me."

Emery came in after the doctor left. "Darling—how are you feeling now? Can you say goodnight to the kids? I parked them at Claudia's while Drake and I went looking for you, and she's just now brought them back."

Bridget held court for a few minutes, lying luxuriously in bed. Mick plucked at her nightgown, but was easily dissuaded. It seemed he was weaned at last, which was a good thing considering that the milk supply would belong to someone else in a few months.

When she tried to get up to go tuck the children in, it turned out that the doctor had left orders she was to stay in bed for 24 hours. Shrugging, Bridget fluffed a pillow.

"You won't get any argument from me," she said to Emery when he herded the children out. "I can't remember the last time I had twenty-four hours in bed. I'm just wondering who's going to keep things running around here."

"I'm not helpless," Emery said loftily. "Don't you worry your pretty little head about it." He turned back at the door with Mick draped across his shoulder, already half asleep. "Claudia has something to say to you. Should she come back tomorrow?"

"Good heavens, no. Send her in," Bridget said grandly.

Claudia was her usual massive, composed self, but she gripped Bridget's hands more tightly than necessary. "Thank goodness you're safe," she said, sitting on the edge of the bed and tilting the matress so that Bridget rolled helplessly toward her. "You could have knocked me over with a feather when Drake said Benji was the killer." She shook her head. "Benji! I wouldn't have thought he could summon the energy to swat a fly, let alone his own aunt."

Bridget shivered. The nightmare of the creek was over, but it would be a while before she could put it away in her thoughts.

Claudia looked at her closely and changed the subject. "I had another reason for being glad you're alive. It would have driven me crazy if you hadn't been around to finish this." She opened her huge handbag and pulled out Bridget's sixty-eight pages of manuscript.

"You liked it?" Bridget took the manuscript diffidently.

"It needs a lot of work, of course." Claudia tapped the pages with a strong finger. "But you have good characters, lots of action—damned if I know what sort of book it'll be, but I believe it's publishable, whatever it is." She fished a notebook out of her bag and scrawled a name and adress on it. "Work it over a little and send what you have to my editor. I'm sure she'll encourage you to finish it."

"Well, lawks a mercy," Bridget said dazedly. "So you think it's good?"

"I said so, didn't I?" Claudia regarded her with exasperated affection. "Now you just have to get busy and finish it up. I don't know exactly how it can be marketed. It isn't really mainstream, and it isn't one of those sparse, literary novels teeming with symbolism and allusion—"

"Thank goodness," Bridget murmured.

"It's not a romance, it's not a mystery—well, I don't know just what it is." Claudia scratched her head and gave up. "Just finish it, will you? I want to see how it ends."

Bridget lay back on her pillows after Claudia left, a bemused smile on her face. She had eight months to finish the book before she had to get ready for the baby. Maybe she would get an advance. Mick could start day care.

Rosy daydreams of seeing stacks of her book piled in the windows at Kepler's were interrupted by Emery again. "You still awake? Paul Drake has some questions for you."

"Sure," Bridget said, tamping down the daydreams. No one knew better than a poet how hard it was to make a living out of words. But for the first time Bridget really felt like a writer, a real writer. "I have a career," she told herself.

"I hope it's not going to be finding bodies." Paul Drake stood by the bed, looking down at her. She couldn't read the expression in his eyes because his glasses caught the light.

"Not at all," she said with as much dignity as her night-gown would let her. Luckily it was the one without holes. "I am a writer, Detective Drake. Didn't you know?"

"Of course." He, too, sat on the bed beside her. She pulled the quilt primly across her chest.

"You're the second woman I've seen tonight propped up in bed, and me without any responsibility for getting or keeping you there." His grin was disarming. "You don't know how out of it that makes me feel."

"So find a woman of your own," Bridget told him. She knew that when Sig heard she was pregnant again, there would be loud railings at fate for giving Bridget a surplus of what Sig wanted so badly.

"Hey, it's not as easy as finding new socks," Drake said, running a hand through his hair. "Tell me what happened tonight, Bridget."

She glanced around. "Aren't you going to tape it? Warn me about—"

"Don't be an ass," Drake said tartly. "You'll have to come to the office and make a formal statement, but for tonight I just need to know what happened, so I can go on from there."

Bridget pointed to her muddy, discarded blue jeans, draped over the wicker hamper next to the bathroom door. "Look in the left-hand pocket," she told Drake. He picked up the jeans gingerly, and pulled out the chin guard.

"Is this it?" He stared down at the bit of plastic, now bent out of shape and scarred by its ordeal in the water.

"I think that's what Martin had in his pocket at the garden—was it just yesterday?" Bridget pushed the hair out of her eyes.

Drake sat on the bed again, staring down at the chin guard. "Tell me what happened."

She started out with the chin guard floating under the bridge and went on without a check until she got to the part about the Grim Reaper's cave.

"What's the matter?" Drake prodded her on.

"I don't know if I should tell you all about that," Bridget confided. "You see, probably they're doing stuff as illegal as hell. But they saved my life. I can't rat on them."

Drake ran his hands through his hair again. "Tell me about it," he suggested. "You can always skip it in your formal statement, or deny you ever said it." She still hesitated, and he sighed impatiently. "I won't bother them, Bridget. I promise. I'm too grateful to them for preventing a fatality to give them any trouble."

Bridget gave in and described the Grim Reaper's inge-
nious method of bringing in the sheaves. She didn't repeat all
the conversation though.

When she got to Benji's revelations, he listened closely.
"That wraps it up," he said at last. "We'll dig up some
evidence now that we know what happened, although it
might not be easy. And it puts you in the clear too." He
smiled at her. "Just in case MacIntyre really does file an
assault complaint against you."

"File an—is he threatening to?"

"He was, last I heard."

Bridget leaned back on her pillows and laughed until she
cried. "I don't know why that struck me as funny," she
apologized, blowing her nose and trying to stop the tears that
streamed down her face.

"Shock," Drake said knowledgeably. "You've had several
over the past week or two."

"You said it." Bridget stared at the footboard of her
ancient bed. "Finding Mrs. Lomax, then Martin, then about
Melanie, and of course the baby—"

Drake seized on Melanie's name. "Tell me about Mrs.
Dixon. Her husband just said she'd gone out of town for a
while last time we called."

"She's doing one of those detox things," Bridget said
absently, her mind suddenly occupied with projecting what
would be happening in nine months or so, when she'd be
holding a new little baby in her arms. She didn't know where
they'd put it, or how they'd handle the increase in the noise
level, or how she'd pursue her newfound career around it.
But she didn't care any more. The thought of its lusty life
pleased her.

"So MacIntyre was the dealer," Paul said to himself. "She
must have been frightened to run like that."

"She did seem scared. She said something about Martin's
death. I wonder if she knew." Bridget wrenched her mind
away from her cuddly speculations and back to the problem

at hand. "She said something about how you could die from it—from addiction to coke."

"She knew something," Drake guessed shrewdly, "but she won't tell any of it. That would make her a witness, and she wouldn't want that."

"Neither would Hugh." They looked at each other. "Well," Bridget said bravely, "I'll be a witness. Guess I'm obligated."

"You sound like it's a dinner party invitation you don't much care for," Drake observed, a muscle twitching beside his mouth. She realized he was trying not to smile.

"Tell you what," she said impulsively, "you and Detective Morales will have to make it up to me. I'll give a real dinner party, after you have all the evidence together. Invite everyone who was concerned. And you two will have to do one of those mystery-story kinds of summing-up, you know? An 'elementary, my dear Watson' type of thing. Are you game?"

Paul smiled at her crookedly and got to his feet. "Certainly, my dear Mrs. Montrose," he said. "If you care to set up the social occasion I'll be happy to—how does it go?— 'give you any other details which might interest you.'"

"Properly Sherlockian," Bridget said with approval. "Pray continue your very interesting narrative, and all that." She extended her hand and he took it for one firm shake, then held it a moment longer, while something more final than a goodnight passed between them.

"Keep in touch, my dear Mrs. Montrose," he said softly, and walked out of her bedroom.

## About the Author
Lora Roberts Smith has worked as a journalist, and writes romances under a pseudonym. She is a transplanted Midwesterner living in Palo Alto with her husband and two young sons. She disagrees with developers who demolish beautiful old houses, but does not recommend murder.

## About the Publisher
Perseverance Press publishes a new line of old-fashioned mysteries. Emphasis is on the classic whodunit, with no excessive gore, exploitive sex, or gratuitous violence.

#1 *Death Spiral, Murder at the Winter Olympics*           $8.95
   by Meredith Phillips (1984)

**It's a cold war on ice as love and defection breed murder at the Winter Olympics. Who killed world champion skater Dima Kuznetsov, the "playboy of the Eastern world": old or new lovers, hockey right-wingers, jealous rivals, the KGB? Will skating sleuth Lesley Grey discover the murderer before she herself is hunted down?**

Reviews said: "fair-play without being easy to solve" *(Drood Review)*, "timely and topical" (Allen Hubin), "surprises, suspense, and a truly unusual murder method" (Marvin Lachman), "Olympic buffs and skating fans will appreciate the frequent chats about sports-lore and Squaw Valley history" *(Kirkus Reviews)*.
Not recommended for under 14 years of age.

#2 *To Prove a Villain*                                     $8.95
   by Guy M. Townsend (1985)

**No one has solved this mystery in five centuries: was King Richard III responsible for the smothering of his nephews, the little Princes, in the Tower of London?**
**Now, a modern-day murderer stalks a quiet college town, claiming victims in the same way. When the beautiful chairman of the English department dies, John Forest, a young history professor beset by personal and romantic problems, must grapple with both mysteries. Then he learns he may be next on the killer's list . . .**

Reviews said: "a mystery set in academe that's wonderfully free from pedantry or stuffiness *(ALA Booklist)*, "a tight, fast-paced tale" *(Louisville Courier-Journal)*, "nicely constructed and unfailingly interesting" (Jon L. Breen), "entertaining and illuminating" (Allen Hubin).

#3 *Play Melancholy Baby*                                            $8.95
   by John Daniel (1986)

**Murder most Californian: murder *in* the hot tub, murder *with* the wine bottle, murder *by* ... ?**

**When the obnoxious piano player is discovered floating face down with a fractured skull, no one has a Clue whodunit. Casey has his hands full already, what with his job (playing old songs in a new world) and new and old loves, not to mention thugs of various nationalities who keep popping up.**

**But the past won't stay dead. When he finds himself in hot water as prime suspect and/or next victim, he realizes it's time to play Sam Spade and dig up some clues. And all he knows for sure is that it wasn't Col. Mustard.**

Reviews said: "readers will thoroughly enjoy the engaging first-person narrative, snappy dialogue, and references to popular music *(ALA Booklist)*, "a mellow mystery with freshly drawn characters—more Woody Allen than Clint Eastwood" (Ralph B. Sipper), "well-written and invigorating" *(The Armchair Detective)*, "I suggest that you 'linger awhile' with this one, for 'this is a lovely way to spend an evening'" *(Santa Barbara Magazine)*.

Not recommended for under 14 years of age.


#4 *Chinese Restaurants Never Serve Breakfast*                       $8.95
   by Roy Gilligan (1986)

**The Monterey Peninsula art world is the background for private investigator Patrick Riordan's brush with death, as he stumbles across the nude, blood-covered body of a promising young painter in her Carmel cottage. On an easel nearby stands an oil painting which exactly depicts the murder scene—and which the artist has neglected to sign.**

**Riordan and his feisty sidekick Reiko chase clues from the galleries and boutiques of Carmel to bohemian studios in Big Sur to the moneyed world of Pebble Beach. The solution? An immutable condition, an inevitable conclusion: Chinese restaurants never serve breakfast.**

Reviews said: "... characters are vivid and sharp ... the

narrator has an engaging, naive charm. Gilligan also conveys the locale effectively" *(Publishers Weekly)*, "a likable sleuth and writing of assured irony" (Howard Lachtman), "fast-paced, detailed and skillful—worthy of a long series" *(Monterey Herald)*, "a likable work, notable for its well-realized Carmel setting, appealing characters, and unpretentiousness" *(The Armchair Detective)*.

#5 *Rattlesnakes and Roses*                                            $8.95
   by Joan Oppenheimer (1987)

**When Kate Regal inherits a fabulous San Diego estate, family resentment turns to murder. She must learn that being tied to the past is as futile as trying to escape from it. The bonds of love, as well as hate and jealousy, are too strong to break—a lesson which puts Kate's life in jeopardy.**

Reviews said: "well-turned-out romantic suspense" (Allen Hubin), "an appealing heroine, a good story, and the perfect book for a quiet Sunday" *(Union Jack)*, "unexpected plot turnings and rich, concise characterization . . . Oppenheimer's natural dialogue and spare, vivid imagery make this an enjoyable, fast-moving story *(Southwest Book Review)*, "well-written, cleverly constructed, and entertaining; recommended *(Small Press)*.

#6 *Revolting Development*                                             $8.95
   by Lora Smith (1988)

#7 *Murder Once Done*                                                  $8.95
   by Mary Lou Bennett (1988)

---

**TO ORDER:** Add $1.05 to retail price to cover shipping for each of these quality paperbacks, and send your check for $10.00 to:

Perseverance Press
P.O. Box 384
Menlo Park, CA 94026

California residents please add 6½% sales tax (58¢ per book).

# By the year 2000, 2 out of 3 Americans could be illiterate.

It's true.

Today, 75 million adults...about one American in three, can't read adequately. And by the year 2000, U.S. News & World Report envisions an America with a literacy rate of only 30%.

Before that America comes to be, you can stop it...by joining the fight against illiteracy today.

Call the Coalition for Literacy at toll-free **1-800-228-8813** and volunteer.

**Volunteer
Against Illiteracy.
The only degree you need
is a degree of caring.**